FEMDOM

Af Her Feet, Surrender to the

Sadistic Domina

PART 2

By

Jessica Ross

FEMDOM PART 2

© Copyright 2020 byJessica Ross

All rights reserved.

This document is geared towards providing exact and reliable information with regards to the topic and issue covered. The publication is sold with the idea that the publisher is not required to render accounting, officially permitted, or otherwise, qualified services. If advice is necessary, legal or professional, a practiced individual in the profession should be ordered.

- From a Declaration of Principles which was accepted and approved equally by a Committee of the American Bar Association and a Committee of Publishers and Associations.

In no way is it legal to reproduce, duplicate, or transmit any part of this document in either electronic means or in printed format. Recording of this publication is strictly prohibited and any storage of this document is not allowed unless with written permission from the publisher. All rights reserved.

The information provided herein is stated to be truthful and consistent, in that any liability, in terms of inattention or otherwise, by any usage or abuse of any policies, processes, or directions contained within is the solitary and utter responsibility of the recipient reader. Under no circumstances will any legal responsibility or blame be held against the

FEMDOM PART 2

publisher for any reparation, damages, or monetary loss due to the information herein, either directly or indirectly.

Respective authors own all copyrights not held by the publisher.

The information herein is offered for informational purposes solely, and is universal as so. The presentation of the information is without contract or any type of guarantee assurance.

The trademarks that are used are without any consent, and the publication of the trademark is without permission or backing by the trademark owner. All trademarks and brands within this book are for clarifying purposes only and are the owned by the owners themselves, not affiliated with this document.

FEMDOM PART 2

Contents

Chapter 15..6
Chapter 16..17
Chapter 17..34
Chapter 18..39
Chapter 19..64
Chapter 20..67
Chapter 21..73
Chapter 22..80
Chapter 23..95
Chapter 24..100
Chapter 25..126
Chapter 26..144
Chapter 27..175
Chapter 28..183
Chapter 29..191

CHAPTER 15

TEMPTATION ISLAND

Regina was still caught between her uncertainty and her own lust.

These games were complicated.

She had the feeling that this agreement benefited Andrew more than her. It had only been about satisfying his lust. It seemed a little unfair to her that she, who was supposed to be in charge, was reduced to a service provider. She would have thought that as a dominatrix would feel a little more delight and excitement.

She craved for sexual pleasure. She yearned for the fulfillment of her savage desires.

Regina had more fun than she had expected, but she hungered like to have more of it. What she was left with were her hands, which disappeared between her thighs after the domination session, was done.

Of course, she could also make Andrew do other things. She could order him to do all kinds of things to satisfy her. She had no doubt that he would like to disappear between her thighs himself. She could imagine how he looked at her lap, where his head rested, which moved rhythmically and created waves of joy in her abdomen.

Regina could well imagine all this.

But she was not like that.

Not so fast, not so brave.

In general, it was not so easy. She didn't just stomp into Andrew's apartment and order around. She needed a plan; she had to think about what she could and couldn't ask for. Regina had to be careful not to overdo it.

Not for Andrew, but for herself and her lustful feelings.

Regina couldn't push Andrew too far. She couldn't expect too much from him either. The story of the incompetent dominatrix Andrew had told her about always remained in the back of her mind as a warning example. It was obviously not so easy being a dominatrix.

Meanwhile, Regina preferred to get used to the term a little more; simply because it was too difficult for her to find an alternative term.

Besides, she also didn't want to stretch too fast. Maybe she was a somewhat rigid, maybe possessing too small-town mentality that compelled her not to immediately press Andrew's head between her thighs and force him to satisfy her. Maybe that's the way they did it in the city, but that's not the way Regina wanted it. She needed time, and she needed a plan.

FEMDOM PART 2

Maybe others could improvise, she wanted to have control over the situation, and that only worked if she knew what she was doing in advance.

It seemed to be a matter of efficiency for Regina to go slowly. Maybe an experienced woman had thousands of scenarios she could play through. Anyway, Regina didn't have them, and she shouldn't run out of ideas. That was to be avoided. So she had to use her resources sparingly.

So the last meeting had been the result of planning. Only this repeated addition wasn't. The order that Andrew shouldn't play around with himself without her permission was her improvisation. Regina wasn't so happy about this, because it meant that she now had his sexuality completely in her hands. She now had to decide when Andrew was allowed to do what. That hadn't been her intention. But now the order was passed and she could hardly roll it back. One day her doorbell would ring and Andrew would ask her for permission to satisfy himself. Regina had no interest in that at all. She could already imagine how he would ring her out of bed in the morning and ask for permission, how she would be disturbed in the cafeteria or during lectures or in the evening when she was having a drink with her friends.

"Let him fiddle with himself! Let him bear the pain of frustration! It was his business," wondered Regina when she went surfing on the internet about taking control of male sexuality and how often a slave should be allowed or just how.

FEMDOM PART 2

On the other hand, it gave Regina an incredible feeling of power over Andrew.

She could determine when he came to the shot, she could deny it to him, she could find ways to please her, and she could even deny Andrew the luxury to please himself according to her moods.

Regina imagined Andrew throwing himself into the dust in front of her, begging and pleading, adoring her and whimpering. How she stood there, enthroned above him. And like an authoritarian empress, like a Queen, she could lift or lower her thumb. She could become the most desirable woman in town. No one would be adored and worshipped like her.

Even that kind of thought triggered an electric pulse deep within her crotch and Regina shivered with excitement. She could feel her heart pounding in her chest.

Regina just didn't know how to put it into practice. She could become the Goddess of submissives men like Andrew, or at least one of them. That was something!

Anyway, she wasn't only responsible for herself, but also for Andrew's feelings. That was what she had to become when she craved to be spontaneous. Regina would have to find a way to deal with it, she thought before turning onto her next plan.

Regina had asked Andrew for five ideas on how he could take his business forward, gain more profits, and incur less loss.

FEMDOM PART 2

In Regina's eyes, Andrew was too spoiled. That wasn't hard to see. And he was too arrogant. "A rather bad character trait," she thought.

"But maybe that's what you need when you're in a better company," Regina concluded.

So she wanted to somehow evaluate and reward or punish each of the five ideas, depending on how excellent or bad she thought they were.

Regina sat down and scribbled down her plan. This was more fun for her than studying, and so she forgot about this list, that she still wanted to learn something.

When she finally went to bed, it was already late, very late indeed than she had actually thought or as per her normal routine. And still, she had to ride a few more waves to come up with an elaborate plan.

When the sun shone in her little room the next morning, Regina snuggled sleepily into her sheets and did what she did damn often in the last few days, more often than she was used to. And when she thought about the dom-sub relationship between her and Andrew, she realized again that Andrew hadn't asked her for redemption yet.

"Was he that disciplined or did he just cheats on me and didn't care about my rules?" Regina wondered breathlessly.

She had a strong feeling that the later was on high probability. She would have to formulate a competent plan to unearth the truth!

FEMDOM PART 2

Regina got up, went into the shower, had breakfast, and then went to the university a little tired and a little unprepared. Her lecture was demanding, but boring. She had to realize that her thoughts were always wandering away from the subject matter that was being educated. In her private life, things happened that were so infinitely more exciting. "Who was interested in SWOT analyses? Strengths, weaknesses, opportunities, and threats?" Regina thought cluelessly as she gazed at the presentation slides in the classroom. These were all terms that she associated with something else, and they were much more exciting!

In the cafeteria, she met two fellow students who had taken an introductory seminar with her. The other two, Michelle and Laura, also came from a small town, even smaller than Regina. But unlike her, they hadn't yet completed their industrial training. They had just graduated from high school although they had much better averages for their career prospects.

Regina got along with them in the first meeting.

Michelle and Laura shared an apartment. They had finished school together and decided to study at the university together. The age difference of three years was immediately noticeable. The two were still playful, hadn't yet got to know the seriousness and boredom of life. They wanted to have fun, they took things easy. When they talked, it was about boys and about fashion trends. They had never worked before and didn't know what it was like to face the industry and deadlines. Did it interfere with their studies? Certainly not. Regina had already understood that their studies had something foreign. No matter how hard one tried to work with concrete determination, in the end, the companies that conducted the campus interviews at the university, had entry-level executives and not respective department heads, who sometimes hired the trainees in garishly dressed up clothes or too loud radios in the coffee kitchen. And the economic problems Regina was dealing with also seemed to be far-fetched.

In any case, Regina had little to do with what she had experienced in practice.

Regina was relieved to have found two like-minded people. It turned out that she herself wasn't the only one who found the whole surrounding of the study extremely complicated. She was not the only one who had a thousand questions about how this or that worked, what had to be considered, and observed at the university. It was similar to both of them. Fortunately, they weren't the same. So Regina had answers to Michelle's questions and she could fill in some of the gaps in Laura's knowledge. So, felt wiser in the end.

So she wasn't alone with her ignorance and didn't feel so stupid anymore. Regina got the confirmation that not she was a bit stupid, but that the system was simply inscrutable. And that was comforting to know. She wasn't alone. There were people like her.

When she cycled home, she had spent much more time with Laura and Michelle than she had planned. Once again, the hours slipped away from her.

On her way back, she passed a small shop.

FEMDOM PART 2

It was called "Plaisirs de la Femme", and under the old-fashioned writing they promised "Toys for the Woman".

A sex shop for women then!

Regina had already cycled past when she realized what kind of shop she had passed, and first, she kept pedaling, because the slogan "Toys for the woman" sounded a bit strange.

Regina involuntarily had to think of scary shaped vibrators that smelled like cheap plastic. Vibrators had always secretly tempted her. But she had never dared to buy one. She would have been extremely embarrassed if anyone found one in her drawer. The pleasure that such a thing promised was definitely less than the embarrassment factor if one should find such a thing in her closet. In general, Regina thought of vibrators as frustrated housewives who needed technical help to have a little more pleasure in life. Vibrators and remote controls for the TV!

But now, Regina no longer lived at home. Now, she had a new apartment and with Andrew. But to sleep with him seemed to be a very, very long way. And definitely, no boyfriend and no brothers would dare to investigate through her drawers.

So it wasn't bad to have a new kinky experience. She was pretty sharp since she was involved off if it would ever happen at all.

Maybe such a vibrator wasn't such a bad idea after all. Regina slowed down, turned around, and drove past the store again. It was a small shop with only one window, and it was sparsely stocked. She couldn't see details in the passing. She turned around again, and now she stopped in front of the shop window. The streets were empty. Nevertheless, she was somehow embarrassed to stop in front of a sex shop for women.

Regina was annoyed about her prudery. This was a city where she didn't know twenty people. "Why am I ashamed anyway?" Regina cursed herself.

In the shop window, there were three vibrators. They looked very stylish, curved, packaged in a discreet box, and had a purple shade. They were designer objects. "But what woman would exhibit her sex toys?" She thought. In the end, surely these pieces were just as much in the drawer as the less chic, flesh-colored ones.

Regina tried to look into the shop, but the decoration made it impossible to look inside. She regretted that but also suspected a conscious decision behind it. "How many women wanted to be seen so easily in a sex shop?" She thought cluelessly again. In general, she liked the business model that women had their own shop where they were among themselves and didn't have to be eyed and harassed by men. "But was the target group big enough? Were there enough women who wanted to visit sex shops?" Regina felt helpless as her agitated mind kept on bombarding questions.

She didn't dare to step in. She just didn't want to look around. "I'm sure I would have a waitress on my hands in no time at all." Regina panicked somewhat. And she would probably have to answer any subtle questions about her masturbation behavior so that someone could sell her the right vibrator.

And because the thought annoyed Regina, she got on her bike and rode on.

Even if she was interested, even if a vibrator wasn't a bad idea, even if she didn't have to fear men, it would still be too embarrassing for her to go into such a shop. She couldn't imagine getting advice in a sex shop about the form and function of vibrators. Possibly from a middle-aged woman with too much make-up and hair dyed too blonde, from a sneaky lesbian maybe. She had nothing against lesbians, for God's sake, no question! But she also didn't want to be advised by someone in a sex shop for women. "God, how prudish could you get?" Regina thought.

So, Regina cycled back, bought some more groceries, and spent the first half of the evening preparing for her university seminar.

But, at some point, her fingers itched too much. Then she grabbed her laptop and searched for vibrators and sex toys in online sex shops. It was all a bit grubby, but also somehow exciting!

And from there, she came to Sado-Masochistic utensils. The more she rummaged in the online shop, the more ideas she got. It was like a flash of inspiration that grabbed her and she threw all kinds of things into her virtual shopping cart. She would give the bill to Andrew after all the stuff was for him.

Regina was excited and a little proud of herself that she had bought sex toys for the first time in her life.

Now, all that had to be delivered discreetly! Not that the stuff would be brought by a short-shaved dyke mailwoman who turned her on right away.

FEMDOM PART 2

CHAPTER 16

TURNAROUND

Three days had passed since she had made Andrew take the vow that he should touch her if he wanted to make out with her. So far Andrew hadn't been in touch. Regina found this unbelievable because the vibrator delivered the day before had already been used. She hadn't yet thought about how she should deal with this matter. "Was he trying to provoke her? Did he want her anger and some kind of punishment? Or had he taken the whole thing less seriously, dismissed it as a game? Or was he not as sharp as she thought he was?" Regina thought cluelessly.

She wasn't sure how to handle it yet.

That afternoon, she had decided to ignore it.

Regina walked confidently through the corridor. She was in a good mood.

"Were you also nice and well-behaved?" Regina asked when Andrew let her into his office. It was an allusion to his phenomenal abstinence.

"Well-behaved?" Andrew questioned.

FEMDOM PART 2

"Good boy. Did you hit your head or why are you so slow?" Regina teased.

"No, no, there's nothing wrong with my head. Good boy. Sounds like one of those puppies." Andrew replied.

"Maybe you are my little puppy?" Regina teased again.

"Should I be your little doggie?" Andrew remarked.

"Would you like to be my puppy?" Regina asked.

"Are we communicating today only in the form of questions?" Andrew was somewhat impatient.

"Are you a little intractable today?" Regina pressed.

"What makes you think so?" Andrew questioned back.

"Because of your many questions," Regina replied.

"I win." Andrew seemed jubilant.

"Won what?" Regina didn't understand.

"Too late!" Andrew chuckled.

"Explain it to me," Regina demanded.

"Because of your many questions. That wasn't a question. Even if the word 'question' appears in it. If we play the 'Ask Me Today' game, I win." Andrew was a bit childish.

"If it makes you happy, I'll let you win," Regina smirked.

FEMDOM PART 2

"Very generous!" Andrew replied.

"What I'm more interested in, is your reference to the puppy." Regina teased again.

"And?" Andrew was curious.

"Would you bark for me once?" Regina smiled wickedly.

"Woof!" Andrew obeyed with a long howl.

"Very nice." Regina laughed. "Maybe I should get you another little collar, one with rhinestones like for a poodle."

"Can't I rather be your Rottweiler?" Andrew sought for a status.

"You are too spoiled for that! You're more the type that eats Sheba all day long." Regina mocked playfully.

"I think Sheba is for cats." Andrew countered.

"Then what do you call this gourmet dog food? Never mind!" She laughed.

Regina sat down in Andrew's executive chair, she put her legs back on the table and folded her arms behind her head.

She was aware of how casual and arrogant she had to arrive at Andrew's place.

Regina liked the way her breasts got lifted up, seemed flatter and shapelier when she raised her arms above her head. Not that she had a problem with her breasts!

FEMDOM PART 2

Andrew had dressed up again, wearing wide linen pants and a light shirt.

She teased about the wide trousers by saying that he probably wanted to be a bit freer in the crotch. But perhaps Andrew also wanted to show himself to her, to make it easier for her to tell whether he was aroused or not.

Andrew also seemed to have been at the hairdresser's, because his hair now lay differently, a little more accurate and orderly. Regina couldn't tell if she liked it more than the casual style he had shown her before. But she was pleased that he tried hard to make a good impression.

She did the same thing, by the way. When she came to see him, she wasn't in her torn jeans and t-shirts. That afternoon, she wore her striped ballerinas and flowered summer dress. It was actually a bit too short for her, didn't even go to her knees, and the fabric was very light and thin so the wind caught it quickly. But in Andrew's office, she was brave enough to wear it, and if he managed to look under her dress, he wouldn't see her everyday underwear, but the better one. Her bra now also matched her panties. These were all precautions. It wasn't that it was planned that she would let him touch the underwear, but she wanted to feel good about herself when she was handling Andrew.

He was again standing a bit indecisively next to his desk.

"Shall we start?" Regina asked.

"With what?" Andrew was a little shocked.

FEMDOM PART 2

"I really don't feel like answering this question. Okay?" Regina rebuffed.

"No topic to discuss then," Andrew asked cluelessly.

"You were going to give me five ideas on how to get your company back on track," Regina commanded.

"I did it!" Andrew swallowed hard.

"Before you start. I'd like to see a little hierarchy here." Regina demanded.

"Okay. What do you want me to do? Go for it." Andrew remarked.

"First, change the tone. Monosyllabic from here on out." Regina dismissed him.

"Monosyllabic?" Andrew couldn't understand.

"It was three syllables!" Regina continued.

"Seriously?" Andrew was curious.

"That's better, it was only two!" Regina remarked.

"Good!" Andrew replied.

"Wonderful!" said Regina, but Andrew went one better.

"Fine!" he smiled provocatively. His answer contained a little sharpness.

FEMDOM PART 2

"Be careful my friend! Do not overdo it! Not another word!" Regina pressed.

Andrew nodded his approval.

"And get down on your knees before me!" Regina commanded.

Andrew nodded again and knelt before her.

Regina liked the sight of him kneeling in front of her and accepting her dominance. And then she had a spontaneous idea, "I think you were a little bit disrespectful. It's okay if we talk to each other, but when it comes to business, I want it to be clear that you recognize my authority and command. How do you see it?"

Andrew nodded his approval again.

"I think it would be an appropriate sign if you kissed my shoes. As a sign of respect." Regina demanded again.

Andrew nodded and crawled on his knees to the desk, leaned forward.

****

Andrew liked this banter between them. But now the thing that really turned him on was his erection throbbing at the mere looks of Regina.

"I see you're hot again. You're like one of those little puppies that can't hold on to anything when it sees a bitch."

FEMDOM PART 2

Regina teased as she glared at his developing tent in between his crotch.

The words burned like a warm whistle in the Siberian steppe. Andrew felt his heart pounding like war drums and he shivered like a leaf in a hailstorm.

"I'd be embarrassed if I were to be always so horny. My feet are enough to give you a hard-on? No wonder you can't make a profit thinking about one thing." Regina chuckled mischievously.

Andrew lowered his eyes to the floor as his excitement started to leak from the tip of his throbbing tool. Regina got down to business pretty quickly. He wasn't like that. He wasn't one of those instinctive leeches. But the situation, the whole situation! He could not help it if Regina rose above him like that, dominated him like that, and enslaved him like that.

"Pardon," he murmured.

"My goodness! You have the self-control of a horny poodle!" Her laughter rattled in his ears.

"Come on, my little one! Kiss my feet! Show me who the boss here is." Regina laughed exuberantly again. "Kiss your domina's feet!"

Andrew obeyed and crawled closer, but when he tried to put his lips on the top of her shoes, Regina began to tap her feet and evaded him.

FEMDOM PART 2

"Why don't you try a little harder!" Regina teased again.

Andrew tried to follow the movement of her feet. But she was too fast, so he couldn't follow the order. Instead, her feet kept pounding roughly against his head.

"Oh, sorry!" she mocked. "Did I hit you?"

She paused, but when Andrew tried to kiss her again, she moved her feet away. She did that a few times until she finally let him kiss her shoes.

****

Regina wondered how disgusting it must be, but a look at his crotch told her that under his trousers everything was still tight.

Andrew enjoyed it!

For a moment, she considered taking off her shoes. Then he could have kissed her feet, but she didn't know what to think about him sticking his tongue between her toes and sucking on her big toe. That went a little too fast for her. She was orthodox about it, and she didn't find her feet the tingliest thing on her body anyway. Although she had no doubt that Andrew would have given a lot of consideration to suck on her toes.

Maybe later!

They had time.

FEMDOM PART 2

Instead, she made fun of him a little, "You're a good little doggie! Go on, give me another woof!"

"Woof!" Andrew howled like a wolf this time.

Regina clapped her hands in delight. She could read in his face how humiliated he was that she let him do such childish things. He did not like it, which was obvious. But she was also sure that it turned him on, that she could demand it of him. That's the way it should be!

"Good doggie! Come closer! Come on. Where's the doggie?" Regina mocked Andrew playfully.

She waved him over with her index finger, and when he was next to her, she patted his head and scratched him under his chin.

Finally, she got cocky, leaned forward, grabbed one of her shoes, and threw it across the room into a corner.

"Retrieve! Get the shoe!" Regina demanded.

Andrew looked at her tortured; the disgraceful humiliation was well evident on his facial expressions, but then he got down on all fours and crawled across the floor to the shoe, picked it up with his teeth, and brought it back to her.

"God, what was she doing to me," Andrew thought. "Did she have to humiliate me like that? With such silly games?" Andrew wondered as he heard his heart pounding like bass drums in his ears. The rancid smell of her foot sweat crept up his nose.

FEMDOM PART 2

Andrew discovered that he had no shoe fetishism. The stench wasn't pleasant. But the situation was. What she could ask of him! How much he made a fool of himself in front of her, just because she wanted him to! He wanted to please her, adore her, worship her and wanted her to be happy with him. And if he had to behave like a dog because she wanted him to, that was the way it was!

When he was back at his desk again, he dropped the shoe on the floor in front of her, and because Regina had so much fun watching him crawl across the floor, she threw her second shoe as well, and he got that one too.

"You're doing really well, and I could do this for hours! But, now we should get down to business. You promised me five ideas. I'm curious." Regina demanded again.

Andrew gazed at her silently, and she peered back piercingly until she got too stupid, "What?"

"May I speak?" he asked.

"What do you think? Will you dance your ideas to me?" Regina asserted.

"I'm just saying. I don't want to violate anything." Andrew was courteous.

"He is getting stroppy now," Regina thought. "Does he want to test me? My authority? But of course, he is right somehow. I had forbidden him more than one syllable."

"I allow you to speak!" Regina said patronizingly.

FEMDOM PART 2

In an instant, his eyes sparkled with enthusiasm. He pulled a few folded sheets of paper out of his back pocket, unfolded them, and began a lecture that was bursting with a verve that had never been thought possible. Unfortunately, Regina understood only half of it. Pretty soon, she realized that she had no idea what such an interior designer was actually doing and that a few glances into the accounts didn't make her a management consultant yet.

Regina had realized that Andrew had acquired new clients, that he was going to change the way he worked, that he wanted to keep in touch more. But to be honest, she didn't really understand what he was up to. Obviously, he thought that after looking at his balance sheets, she was a precise connoisseur of his company. In fact, she wasn't. But she also didn't want to ask questions or expose her ignorance. So she listened, nodded, asked a few questions here and there, which sounded intelligent and should prove that she listened attentively. But actually she didn't listen, because it was terribly boring. She would have rather play with him and let him fetch her shoes.

To be honest, Regina expected something like this on the five points:

One, he would take his business more seriously.

Two, he'd be more careful about his spending.

Three, he wouldn't buy so much crap.

Fourth, he'd get more customers.

FEMDOM PART 2

Five, he'd just try harder.

But Andrew had really thought about it in great detail to convince his customers and above all, make a good impression on Regina. That was nice, but she wasn't even interested that day.

But, it was all right that Regina had to go through that.

She suppressed a yawn.

Andrew was still kneeling in front of her, but the playful mood soon evaporated. A look at his crotch told her that his blood was circulating in his brain; at least it was no longer in his loins.

Regina's plan had sounded more interesting. Andrew had kneeled before her while she was sitting in the desk chair. He was supposed to keep his thighs apart, and she had planned to play with her foot between his crotch while he presented his ideas. She would have rewarded good ideas by stroking his crotch with her foot, and if it was a bad idea, she would have exerted a little pressure, perhaps kicked lightly between his legs. Not to cause him real pain, but to scare him a little and show him her domineering possibilities. Regina could have massaged his crotch so softly and gently, and perhaps kicked Andrew a moment later to show him how unpredictable she was.

Regina had imagined it all so beautifully and excitingly. But now she was maltreated with a boring lecture.

Regina sighed inwardly.

FEMDOM PART 2

****

Andrew sprayed with verve. Anyway, he was in his formidable domain. It wasn't quite his own domain, he had to admit. His plans were primarily those of his father's accountant. Mr. Donnie, his father's accountant had once given him some well-intentioned suggestions on how to become more profitable. Andrew had put that down in the 'need to pee' category. But now he had an incentive, and he realized that the ideas weren't so bad after all. He had spent the whole of the previous day rethinking, analyzing, and working it all out. "Now, she should praise me." Andrew wondered enthusiastically. He had endeavored to make an impact.

Anyway, Andrew was in his domain and talked and babbled and lectured and didn't realize how much he bored Regina.

When he was finally finished, he stared at Regina expectantly. But Regina had difficulties to give a serious feedback and so she said indefinitely, "Altogether not bad. At this one point, you still have to work on, it still has weaknesses. But you are on the right track!"

It was as concrete as she could get, and as distant as she could get. Of course, Regina also had no idea what this 'one point' was that Andrew was still working on. But she didn't want to get too euphoric either. A query from Andrew curtly suppressed her. Instead, she had a spontaneous idea, "I want you to write all of this down for me again in great detail. I saw that you have a small storage room in your apartment."

"You mean the one where the cleaning lady keeps her stuff?" Andrew was somewhat baffled.

"That's the one. I want you to clean it out, and then write everything down. Naked. I don't want you to have a piece of cloth on you when you write this down. Understood?" Regina commanded.

Andrew nodded, but his uncomprehending expression compelled her to explain, "You're too spoiled for me with your fat apartment and your fat office and all your luxuries. You need to learn some humility. Therefore nice and naked with paper and pencil in the storeroom! Understood?"

"Yes, I understand," Andrew swallowed hard.

"And one more thing. The closet stays just the way it is. You don't buy furniture for it. You don't wallpaper or tile it, or do anything with it, except clean it first. And you do that yourself. Not your cleaning lady. Understood?" Regina asserted.

"Yes, I think I'm," Andrew replied.

The addition of the forbidden redecoration of the storage room was more of a joke, but Andrew's disappointed expression showed that in the few moments of passing this order, his agitated mind was already vibrant with some ideas.

FEMDOM PART 2

Anyway, Regina could surmise in Andrew's enthusiasm that her idea hadn't been completely wrong.

"One more thing!" Regina spoke sternly.

He looked at her in a dejected way.

"You remember my order. I do not want you to play with yourself in the chamber. Is that clear?" Regina asked.

Andrew nodded his approval.

"Is that clear?" Her voice was cutting metal across the room.

"Clear." Andrew acknowledged. He looked depressed.

Regina was pleased. She decided to give him at least one more piece of candy.

"You didn't do badly. As a reward, you may kiss my feet. Each toe separately. But no tongue!" Regina demanded.

Andrew nodded, and in his eyes, she saw gratitude. She took her feet off the desk so that he would have to bow cordially before her.

Andrew crawled at her feet and bowed down before her.

His hungry lips felt warm on her feet. Slowly and carefully he placed a kiss on each of her toes. Regina felt chills gushing down her spine; her heart was beating a thousand times faster than normal.

FEMDOM PART 2

It tickled a little and while he followed his work, Regina wondered how her toes must have affected him. It flashed through her mind that she should have had a pedicure. But now it was too late and maybe she just had to relax a little bit concerning her body. Until then, no one had ever kissed her feet.

When Andrew changed from her left to her right foot, he took his time, which wasn't wrong for Regina. She could even enjoy the gesture, adoration, and submission. Here a man lay at her feet and kissed her toes like she was a Goddess.

"Didn't every woman wish for a man who carried her on his hands? Who took care of her?" Regina wondered breathlessly.

She had found one who even kissed her feet, and enjoyed the ordeal to shower his heartfelt tributes.

If she told anyone, nobody would believe her. But who would she tell?

Her friends in her hometown would have no understanding at all, would call it perverted, as she had done herself until a few days ago. Regina thought of Michelle and Laura, her fellow students, but she didn't know them well enough to entrust them with such dirty little secrets.

When Andrew looked up at her again, she had put on an elated expression and said, "Ready? You seem to have gotten off on it!"

FEMDOM PART 2

It seemed to her as if he flinched a little under her words.

"That was okay. He should." Regina wondered. She was pleased.

FEMDOM PART 2

Chapter 17

REWORK

Andrew cowered in the storeroom.

Naked.

He had emptied it all by himself and found the cleaning products whose purpose was obscure to him. Before that, he had taken a photo with his iPhone to record what was where, because obviously he would have to put everything back when he was done.

Once Andrew had had the absurd idea of getting his excitement out of his jeans, and due to a lack of alternatives he had rummaged around in the storeroom and tried out various remedies. Maria, the cleaning lady, had freaked out and reproached him with her ponderous accent. She had screamed and cursed, partly in Polish, and he couldn't make sense of why it was such a big deal. In the retrospective, he wondered whether her resolute appearance had already excited him at that time, just as he was now always put into a state of horniness by Regina when she showed her dominance.

But he hadn't felt that way back then. Maybe it was because Maria was in her late fifties and rather chubby, and she didn't always have her personal hygiene under control. To be more precise, her deodorant sometimes failed enormously. But he had to hire her because his father wanted her to. Maria was the wife of someone, a former cleaning employee of his father, who had fallen off the scaffolding or something. He had no choice.

So, Andrew cowered in the storeroom.

Naked, as Regina had ordered him.

And he was always aware of the missing clothes so that he didn't achieve much concentration. He was just focused on the cool air on his crotch and the throbbing of his achingly hard erection and the situation he was in. That he would stoop to someone like that just because she asked him to!

The words Andrew wrote down on the pad were incoherent and he would have to endure the unbearable shivering all over his aroused body every second in a presentable way.

Andrew had noticed that Regina hadn't been as attentive as he had expected and he had also noticed that she hadn't understood everything he had explained to her. That was no wonder. His business was no child's play. He saw himself as a highly professional expert. So he couldn't expect that such an amateur student who had learned to add up a few numbers would even begin to understand his ideas.

And yet, following Regina's instructions, Andrew sat in a storeroom and tried to make her understand what he meant by his explanations and analysis and how he could cooperate with his father's company. Moreover, everything was done in an extremely humiliating position and him constantly horny and unable to grasp a clear thought.

He simply couldn't concentrate.

In the end, Andrew had to make a decision.

He had to get his hormonal balance under control; otherwise, he would never finish, couldn't carry out her order, and wouldn't satisfy her.

Andrew had to disregard one of her orders in order to follow others. There was no other way, he thought and wondered about Regina, and how she made him cower under her sheer dominance and authority, the smell of her intoxicating body and jerked off to an intense orgasm.

All the time he had in mind was how she stood in the door frame, her arms on her hips, barefoot and he was at her mercy. How she made him kiss her feet, how he looked up at her.

When Andrew was able to control himself again, he felt extremely cold and depleted. He studied his notes, found that they were almost finished, and decided to finish the job in the storage room. He didn't want to catch a cold in that chilled room with no clothes on. Besides, he would be finished faster and more orderly if he could do the fair copy at a table. He decided that this was certainly in Regina's mind, too, so he left the storeroom, put on some clothes, and quickly and somewhat sloppily put the room back in.

He would bear the wrath of his cleaning lady.

FEMDOM PART 2

Then Andrew sat down at his laptop, wrote a few more emails, and made an appointment with one of the new clients he had been trying to find. It was easier to do business than he had thought if he hung in a little.

****

Meanwhile, Regina sat at her little kitchen table and learned. The previous evening had taught her two things:

First: She knew less about business than she thought. It seemed to her to be inevitable to acquire more knowledge. She couldn't play the dominatrix on the one hand and on the other hand, she couldn't understand anything about all the things she was being paid for.

Her work ethic forbade her to dabble. It also seemed to be detrimental to her authority if she had no knowledge of the things she claimed to know.

Such a venal dominatrix had it easier; she had to have no idea of the things her clients earned their money with. She could focus on her dominance. But since Regina was new in this area as well, she didn't want to expose herself anymore. So she had to cram, and so she first studied for university and then made herself familiar with the restructuring of sick companies, read about economic rationalization measures and other things.

Only when Regina got a headache did she go to bed. By then it was already quite late, and before she fell asleep, she reviewed the game with Andrew.

FEMDOM PART 2

This little interlude with the naked writing down of his ideas in the storeroom had been excellent. She imagined Andrew sitting there and following her orders.

And yet his motivation still remained alien to her. She didn't understand him, she didn't understand the man.

At school, Regina had had to read a play by Max Frisch. It was called Don Juan, but Don Juan in the play was an involuntary crush on women. In this play, there was a sentence pronounced by Don Juan that had interested her:

"Every man has something greater than a woman when he sobers up."

In her experience with men, Regina had often heard this sentence. She had made the experience that her ex-boyfriends became aroused much more quickly when making love, but also lost interest much more quickly than she did. If her last ex-boyfriend had come during sex, it only took seconds and he had lost all interest in her.

No cuddling, no after play. Just a moment ago, he might have been full of ecstasy; a moment later he rolled out of bed and asked Regina if she wanted some fried eggs, too. It was unbelievable how quickly all his excitement disappeared.

"Was it the same with Andrew? Did his candle burn even brighter and even shorter than the one of her ex-boyfriends?" Regina wondered cluelessly.

She'd find out.

FEMDOM PART 2

CHAPTER 18

SECURITY MEASURES

"I'm a little worried!" Regina glared.

"About what?" Andrew was confused.

Regina had just rung his doorbell. It was already after ten o'clock. Andrew was bored in front of the TV. The channel telecasted a Bundesliga game, but he didn't pay attention to it. Instead, he surfed with his laptop and sipped his red wine again and again. A client wanted fancy textile wallpaper, so he researched patterns. At the same time, he scribbled on a pad because he needed ideas for furnishing an apartment. Actually, artistically and completely uninteresting for Andrew, but it just brought in money and he had committed himself to the idea of no longer making losses but standing on his own legs.

So now Andrew had to jump over his shadow.

He was well aware of the irony that this path led through the people who wanted to make contact with his father. The person that he wanted to emancipate himself from... But that was the way it was. "You couldn't have everything," Andrew sometimes wondered and found it irresponsible to ignore these people who wanted to throw their money at him. In this case, there were even big deals on the horizon, because the businessman, who ran a small chain of hotels, nothing big. But at least he wanted to have his living room redecorated by Andrew. Actually, he wanted to make himself popular with Andrew's father in order to build some new hotels on the outskirts of several middle-sized cities in a partnership business with him. And that's when Andrew came into play again because there was a vague prospect that he could take over the furnishing. They were to be modern design hotels.

Just the term alone made his mouth water. Although Andrew was actually aware that it would be a pretty big job, far bigger than anything he had undertaken so far. And Andrew had to admit that he had no idea how to tackle such a project because one thing was completely different from the orders of privateers he had been dealing with so far. With them, money was no problem. On the contrary, they were even interested in showing that they had it and could spend it. But the hotels were something else. They wanted things to look classy but had to be cheap. They didn't make money in luxury; they made money by making it look like it. That was a different kind of work.

Those were the questions he was concerned with, anyway. But with all of them at the same time, which didn't exactly have a positive effect on the quality of his work. It was playing around; a waiting for inspiration, for a flash of inspiration, and it was a long time coming.

Andrew was all the more grateful when the doorbell rang unexpectedly.

FEMDOM PART 2

Regina stood there and immediately Andrew was wide awake.

He hadn't expected her.

"I think you should give me a key", Regina said. "I do not think it is appropriate to have to wait outside the door."

"Of course", Andrew answered without much enthusiasm, for his privacy was already important to him.

She entered without asking, went into his living room, and sat on the couch. In her hand, she had something like a toilet bag, which she casually placed beside her.

"I'd love a glass of wine like that!" Regina demanded.

"Of course!" Andrew replied and went into the kitchen to bring her a glass. He poured her a glass and felt like a waiter.

Regina took it without paying any attention to him.

"To what do I owe the honor of your visit?" Andrew asked.

"Am I disturbing you?" Regina asked back.

"No, no!" he repulsed! "I only mean!"

"I intended to give you a little company. But if it's not convenient, I'll leave." Regina remarked.

"No, no! For God's sake! You're not disturbing me." Andrew pleaded.

FEMDOM PART 2

"You just have to say so." Regina pretended she wanted to get back up.

"I beg you!" He walked towards her with his arms outstretched as if he wanted to beg her.

"That's nice of you to think so!" Regina teased.

Regina crossed her legs and enjoyed her superiority.

"You have been so obedient until now and did everything I asked of you. That was certainly not always easy!" Regina asserted.

Andrew nodded in agreement, even if he secretly couldn't say what great privations or torments he had suffered so far. But in fact, he felt that he had behaved in an exemplary manner.

"That is why I wanted to reward you! What do you think of that?" Regina remarked playfully.

"I think that's very generous of you," Andrew replied.

"Very generous, indeed! I think that's sweet of you to say!" Regina teased.

"Was she making fun of me?" Andrew couldn't say for sure. He could hardly believe his luck.

"There's just one thing." Regina paused for a moment.

"What do you mean?" Andrew was somewhat startled.

FEMDOM PART 2

"I'm a little worried!" Regina wondered.

"About what?" Andrew was curious.

"About your libido." Regina mocked.

"My what?" Andrew was baffled.

"Your libido. Your sexuality. Your horniness." Regina exclaimed.

"Don't worry. There's nothing wrong with me." Andrew replied.

"That's what I worry about. If I'm making you horny, what guarantee do I have that you won't jump on me?" Regina sounded worried.

"I would never do anything like that! You ought to know me that well!" Andrew countered.

"That's just it. I don't know you that well. I don't know what you're like or what you're like when you're horny! Maybe you turn into a libertine!" Regina rebuffed.

"Was she serious? I had been a perfect gentleman until now." Andrew wondered inwardly. "You really don't need to worry!"

"If only I could! But you will understand that I cannot trust you. I mean, you have strange tendencies. I mean, what man wants to be treated like dirt by women. I wouldn't call it normal!" Regina argued.

FEMDOM PART 2

So it hit Andrew that Regina called him a pervert. But he didn't know what to say to that, so he kept quiet.

"To make a long story short... I'm sure we'll get it right in no time. All I'm asking for is a little protection. Just to be safe." Regina explained.

So she opened the toilet bag and pulled out some handcuffs. They were covered with plush!

"I had them sent over along with some other stuff. I'll get you the bill. Nothing dramatic." Regina dangled her handcuffs invitingly in front of his face.

"What did you say? A little security." Regina joked.

What could Andrew reply except, "Yes! Of course! Of course not, although I understand that my manhood is giving you a headache."

Andrew wasn't quite sure how much irony there was in that statement. A little, certainly, but maybe not as much as one might expect. Andrew didn't want to cast doubt on his manhood. There must have been a bunch of smart men, philosophers, commanders, and dictators who enjoyed playing games similar to his. He didn't have to justify himself! He was a man like any other. It was just that he had this one predilection.

But Andrew didn't mind the handcuffs. On the contrary. The very sight of them excited him again.

FEMDOM PART 2

"I'm glad you agree," Regina stated. She threw the handcuffs at him, but they were too short so they fell on the floor in front of him.

"Couldn't she throw them, or was that on purpose?" Andrew wondered and bent down and picked up the handcuffs.

"Oops! Sorry!" Regina said in an emphatically girlish voice. "Sorry!"

Well, he could have guessed that.

"Why don't you take one of the chairs from the dining table and put it here?" Regina demanded.

She pointed to the middle of the living room and he brought the chair.

"Sit down," Regina commanded.

Andrew obeyed.

"Now put the handcuffs on, behind the backrest." Regina was stern as usual.

Andrew swallowed once, and then he obeyed. He didn't expect to be handcuffed again that night. He sat down on the chair and a strange thought flashed through his mind, "How reckless is this? What I just did? I gave myself over to her." Once he was tied up in the chair, she could do anything to him. He had to think of his precarious dominatrix.

FEMDOM PART 2

This was strange for him because he hadn't had this thought of being at the mercy of others when he had visited this Mistress Angela. It had never occurred to him to worry too much, although he had limped away with bruised buttocks in the end. But it wasn't only that. It was rather the fact that Regina was of a different caliber. Regina was unpredictable, she was terrifying to him, and she played with him. She was great! Andrew really had to be afraid of her. She might not beat his ass, but she was cunning and dangerous. He was into her, and he loved it!

But these thoughts came to him later, when it was too late, if he so chose.

At that moment, after some fiddling, the handcuffs clicked behind his back and sealed his fate.

Although Andrew was now handcuffed, Regina remained sitting on the couch, legs crossed, and an unfathomable smile.

She looked so sexy. A conniving hussy in the guise of a harmless dominatrix.

Andrew had no idea what was coming.

He didn't trust her words anymore, but he trusted her.

Regina was now the woman of his dreams.

Andrew was eager to know where his journey would take him.

So was Regina.

FEMDOM PART 2

****

She was a little astonished how easy it was, how docile he was. Men were generally considered to be hormone controlled, but that it was so easy!

Slowly Regina stood up. She had the toilet bag in her hand.

Andrew's eyes lay on her, greedy and full of desire, but also a little worried. After all, he had surrendered himself to her, sat there tied up and helpless in front of her.

Regina didn't take her eyes off Andrew. She was very aware of her movements, of every single one. She felt like a woman. That was not new, but now it was different.

Never before had a man desired her so much as at this moment. At least, that's what she suspected. It seemed to her that she had never had to do so little to turn a man on before.

It was all right with her. Regina loved to be desired, and she liked to be sexy.

She walked slowly towards Andrew, her hips swinging a little more than they should with every step.

Andrew kept his eyes on her. He was getting hypnotized.

"You're reckless," Regina breathed into his ear.

"Why?" Andrew gulped hard.

FEMDOM PART 2

"I can do anything with you now!" Regina whispered. Her warm breath shot jolts of thunder across his shivering body.

"Please do it. Do anything. Do anything to me." Andrew pleaded desperately.

"You shouldn't get greedy, and you shouldn't get reckless. Who knows what I'm going to do with you." Regina teased.

She stepped behind him so he couldn't see her anymore. She gently stroked his hair.

"I want to see you," Regina whispered into his ear. She took the toilet bag and took out a small pair of nail scissors.

"Of course!" Andrew sounded enthusiastic.

"I'm sorry, you still have your shirt on." Regina chuckled deviously.

She held the nail scissors up to his face and then to the top button.

"Expensive shirt?" Regina asked.

"Made to measure," Andrew replied.

"Then maybe we should stop it all and call it off." Regina teased wickedly.

"No, no, no, no, no, no, no, no, no, no, no, no, no. Cut it open if you want." Andrew was desperate for the toy.

FEMDOM PART 2

"Are you sure? The expensive shirt." Regina was toying with his mind like he was in the devil's lair.

But Regina didn't wait for his answer. She cut the thread and the button flew through the room in a high arc and fell clattering somewhere in the corner.

She did the same with the next ones until his shirt was completely open. She stepped in front of him, bent over to him until their faces were very close together. Andrew already thought she wanted to kiss him, but instead, she pulled the shirt over his shoulders with all her strength. The tearing of the seams cut across the entire room.

"I brought my toilet bag. You've already seen the scissors," Regina said. "When traveling, you always have to wash. She pulled out two clothespins, opened and closed them in front of Andrew's eyes, and then she put one on Andrew's left nipple. When she closed, Andrew hissed in pain.

"I don't want to hear you moan," Regina said sternly, and Andrew tried to control himself as the second clip bit into his right nipple.

Regina took a step back and looked at Andrew.

"You know, I have a little bit of a feeling that you're not being honest with me!" Regina demanded.

"What makes you think that?" Andrew moaned as he felt the agony of the clothespin crushing on his nipples.

FEMDOM PART 2

"I've ordered you not to tamper with yourself without my permission. Remember that?" Regina was stern.

Andrew nodded.

"I don't know about you, but I'm already having trouble keeping my fingers on me, and I'm allowed to. I don't have to ask anybody's permission! I can use my five friends anytime I want!" She held her right hand in front of his face, kissed her middle finger, and placed it gently on his lips.

"When I see how sharp you are, I wonder how you can stand it." Regina teased mischievously.

Andrew didn't know whether he should answer. He decided to remain silent.

"You're not saying anything! But I think its better that way." Regina reached back into her toilet bag and pulled out a terry cloth washcloth and waved it back and forth in front of Andrew's eyes.

"I use it to cleanse my body. You know where it's been?" She laughed, vaguely suggesting she washed between her legs with it, she cleansed her rosebuds. It was a vulgar movement, but she wanted to be vulgar at that moment.

Andrew's mind was so excited that for a moment he thought it was going to explode.

She surprised him a little with her frankness.

FEMDOM PART 2

Regina rolled up the cloth and stuffed it into Andrew's mouth.

"So you don't talk so much!" Regina chuckled wickedly.

Andrew snorted through his nose.

"But back to the topic! How do you stand it with your hormones?" Regina questioned sternly.

She snapped her finger against one of the clothespins on his nipple.

The pain, which had subsided to a dull throb, returned immediately.

"Or can't you stand it at all because you're doing it to yourself on a whim?" Regina mocked him.

Andrew looked at her with big eyes, happy not to be able to answer.

"Because I have some doubts about your willingness to accept my authority. How can I trust you when you can so brazenly betray me?" Regina asserted.

Andrew didn't answer.

"So, what's the situation? Am I right? Oh, you better not say anything." Regina was toying with a puzzled Andrew.

She walked slowly and silently around him, like a wild cat circling her prey.

FEMDOM PART 2

"I still have a few things in my toilet bag!" Regina asserted.

She pulled out a pretty red lipstick. Regina had bought it once. It was even expensive but much too bright. It did not fit her. But it was enough to rub in Andrew's face.

Regina held the thing in front of his face.

"You could use a little color, I think!" Regina teased again.

Andrew struggled, tried to turn his head away when Regina came closer, but she grabbed him roughly by the hair and fixed his head.

"Not so unruly!" Regina demanded.

She pressed the lipstick hard on his mouth and smudged it. Andrew looked disgusted and tried to make his lips small.

Regina was astonished by how much Andrew resisted.

"What are you trying to do? I make you pretty as if you're my little friend!" Regina remarked teasingly.

Andrew shook his head in shock.

"Don't you like it?" Regina laughed. "Won't you be my little slut?"

Regina recognized his disgust. He seemed not to be acting. But that was what turned her on.

FEMDOM PART 2

"If you are so reluctant, then I will do it all the more! The more you bitch, the longer I play around with you! Do you know why?" Regina questioned playfully.

Andrew shook his head.

"Because I can do it! And there's nothing you can do about it!" She laughed.

Regina tossed her lipstick around a bit. Andrew looked quite ridiculous, sitting there with red, smeared lips. But she wasn't finished yet.

Regina rummaged in her toilet bag and found her rouge. She folded the lid up and generously spread too much rouge on his cheeks with a brush.

Andrew shook his head again and reared up against his shackles and tugged at his handcuffs.

Regina saw how his muscles tightened. The two clothespins danced on his nipples as he moved. That must have hurt!

Andrew still looked quite fit for his age.

But now it was enough for Regina and without thinking she gave him a hard slap which was more reverberating than she had intended.

"Stop it now!" she reigned over him.

Regina herself was shocked by the resonating noise she had made and her hand was burning. It had not been her intention to hurt him. Her handprint impression was clearly visible on his cheek.

Andrew stared at her silently. She could see the tears pooling up in the corner of his eyes.

In his eyes, Regina found respect, maybe even a little fear.

Regina had hit a nerve with Andrew. She assumed that it was the feminization that made him react. But it could also be his bondage.

"Don't be such a baby," she yelped. "And now keep still. A little more eyeliner to accentuate your beautiful eyes and you'll look totally cute!"

Andrew held really still as she made his eyes, though he stared at her angrily as if his eyes were glowing daggers. But stoically Regina ignored this. When she was finished she took a step back and proudly said, "Now look at you! Like an adorable little lady!" She clapped her hands in delight, took out her makeup mirror, and held it up to Andrew's face. He grunted angrily.

"Don't you like it?" Regina asked with feigned anxiety. "Oh, it will be alright. I think you look wonderful! We should record this for eternity!"

She pulled out her iPhone and took some photos.

"Wonderful!" She laughed again. "Who knows who we can show them all to!"

FEMDOM PART 2

Regina looked at the photos and then showed them to Andrew, who could only grunt into the gag.

Then she went back to the sofa and sat down and crossed her legs.

So far everything had gone according to plan, but now the finale was to come! She was excited.

But first, she enjoyed the moment.

Andrew with terrycloth washcloths in his mouth, hands tied behind his back, two clothespins on his nipples and dressed up like a crazy lady.

The sight was divine!

Regina took out her cell phone once more, directed him a little, and took a few pictures.

"Smile! ... That's it! ... Head to the left! That's it." Regina joked.

Andrew looked at her with a scowl.

Finally, she put her cell phone away again and said, "I still don't know how you keep it in check like that. You haven't asked me once for permission to come. I think that either shows considerable self-discipline or that you are betraying me. What do you think?"

Andrew grunted incomprehensibly.

FEMDOM PART 2

"But I'm generous for once and I suppose you really do have that much self-control." Regina teased playfully.

She looked at him, but Andrew just stared back blankly.

One answer would only sabotage her plan because her goal was something else. She went on, "And that's why I want to reward you! Yes, you heard right. I want to reward you! You have been really good these last days. You have done everything I wanted you to do, you never complained. Then you made those nice restructuring and designing plans. They sound really good! It can't have been easy." Regina was trying to sound a little condescending.

"I think you deserve a reward for that. I think you deserve a reward. What do you think?" Regina asserted teasingly.

She looked at him and said he didn't know what to think.

"Or don't you want a reward?" She played with Andrew, and he shook his head at once.

"No, you don't want a reward?" Regina teased again.

She pretended to be disappointed and ignored his violent nodding at first.

"Now you do want your reward?" Regina remarked playfully.

Andrew nodded more heavily and grunted into the gag.

"Are you sure? You don't seem very convincing!" Regina coyly said.

FEMDOM PART 2

Andrew kept nodding.

"All right, then. Then you shall have your reward! Do you think you can get up from that chair?" Regina remarked playfully.

Andrew slowly rose from the chair and tried to lift his arms above the backrest.

"Beware," she admonished him with feigned anxiety.

Andrew stopped once, but in the end, he had freed his arms and was now standing. His hands were still tied behind his back, though.

"Bravo! You've done well!" Regina clapped her hands as if she was really proud of him.

"But I like it better when you're on your knees. It symbolizes our relationship more appropriately, don't you think?" Regina chuckled wickedly.

Andrew got down on his knees.

"Don't fall down." Regina admonished.

He did not.

"Now come a little closer. Right here." She pointed at her feet.

It was tedious for him to crawl forward step by step, and it looked ridiculous, but Andrew did it. It wasn't the first time he had done it.

FEMDOM PART 2

"That's a good boy." Regina smiled with feigned leniency and took a short break. The next order should come out perfectly. She was a bit excited herself, which was silly, really.

"I think you deserve an orgasm." Regina teased.

She saw his eyes widen.

"Are you excited?" Regina asked playfully.

Regina waited for his nod.

"I hope you don't think we sleep together!" She laughed as if she thought the thought herself absurd. "But you deserve a little orgasm, I think!"

She paused, and then said, "You may begin."

Andrew was confused. His arms were tied behind his back and he was kneeling on the floor. He looked at her questioningly.

"You don't think I'm going to lay a hand on you, do you? I don't want your grease on my hands afterward." Regina remarked wickedly.

Andrew shrugged his shoulders.

"But because you're such a good little puppy, a poodle, when I look at your make-up, I let you do it like little dogs in heat!" Regina put her left leg out.

"You can rub against this!" Regina demanded.

FEMDOM PART 2

Andrew gazed at her absolutely baffled at her commands.

"Like a little doggie!" Regina teased mischievously.

Regina was caught up in her game that she herself was incredibly aroused. She never thought she could feel so much joy in humiliating someone. It almost scared her a little. But not at this moment. At that moment, the overbearing patronizing was carved into her face. She was a bitch, and she knew it. It was like black blood coursing through her veins, infecting her with randy malice. Like a wild horse that she had lost control of and carried from one viciousness to another. She could do nothing but hold on to his raven black mane and enjoy his strength and power.

Andrew looked at her in horror. But she also recognized his excitement.

He should rub his erection on her leg for an orgasm!

She looked at him and saw how humiliating it must be for him.

"You know that everything is different between us after this? When you humiliate yourself like this in front of me." Regina stated.

Andrew looked at her for a long time and then nodded.

"This is not a game anymore. I'm subjugating you. You don't have to do it. But if you do, then you and I will know forever what happened here. Then you made yourself my doggy." Regina asserted.

FEMDOM PART 2

Andrew nodded.

"Your makeup can be wiped off, photos deleted. But this thing here stays! We'll both always know that you jerked off on my leg!" Regina spoke sternly.

He nodded as he heard his heart pounding like war drums. He could feel the shivers transforming into goosebumps.

"If you want to, go ahead!" Regina teased.

It took a lot of effort. Regina enjoyed it. Her heart was beating and her clit was throbbing.

Then Andrew crawled slowly forward. It was still tiring.

Regina bent her leg a little.

He was now close to the couch, his legs already between hers. He looked at her again as if he wanted to give her another chance to change her mind, maybe to lean forward to him and kiss him passionately.

They could roll over the floor. Regina would still have all power over him, bound as he was. But did Andrew prefer that than the humiliation he was about to experience?

Regina looked at her leg. It was freshly shaved and creamed. She was prepared.

Andrew now touched her shin. Regina felt his erection. It was strange. Andrew slipped forward a little bit and then he had found his position. Slowly and carefully he moved his hips forwards and backward, rhythmically exerting pressure on her leg with his throbbing. He moved slowly.

Regina thought that was good. Andrew should enjoy it. On the other hand, the warmth of his erection had stimulated her rosebuds. The dominance was burning her and enkindling the buried lust in her.

But in the next moment, he picked up speed. He had bent over and was busy with himself. Regina sensed that it would all happen quickly. He puffed heavily into the gag.

But Regina couldn't let him experience his climax without her. So she reached into his hair and pulled up his head and stared into his eyes. Her eyes locked together, and she wouldn't let go of him. She wanted him to know who he had to thank her for it expressed his gratitude to her. After all, she was one who controlled him.

Andrew's movements became instantly faster, the grunting louder. He gasped like a horny boar.

Regina stared at him, still holding his hair in her right hand. When she felt that he was close to the climax, she gave him a sign with her eyes, and in the next moment, the climax washed over him with a liberating grunt. She could feel the veins pulsating as they shot into delightful liberty, some droplets crashed on her feet and the warmth of the juice only coupled her excitement. Regina tore his head back roughly and with her other hand she knocked off the clothespins that were still stuck to his nipples. The sudden pain, when the blood ran into his numb nerves, made him scream, muffled by the cloth in his mouth, which was still so loud that Regina wondered if the neighbors had overheard him.

And during all this, they both stared at each other and Regina had the feeling as if she had stolen his soul as if he now belonged to her.

In the end, he collapsed on top of her completely exhausted. Her dress had slipped up, and his chest was now warm on her thigh. She felt his chest rise and fall. His head lay in her lap. Through the thin dress, she felt his heavy breath.

Regina let him have this moment and stroked his hair like a child being comforted.

"Did he need consolation? He had given himself to her, after all." Regina wondered inwardly.

The two of them lay there for a few more moments.

When Andrew had regained some of his strength, Regina rolled him away and stood up.

He didn't want to look at her, left his head on the sofa.

It was all right for her.

Regina took out the keys to the handcuffs, opened them, and threw them carelessly on the floor.

She stood a little indecisively above him. She had planned everything so beautifully, and it had all become such a great reality.

FEMDOM PART 2

One last time she reached into his hair and turned his head towards her, but this time gently and motherly.

"We both know what just happened here," Regina breathed softly.

Andrew nodded.

"Good!" she said, unlocking his handcuffs and then leaving his apartment.

As she walked out, she felt the moisture on her shin that his climax had left on her.

FEMDOM PART 2

CHAPTER 19

TRUE MALE

Andrew was already a little worried about what was going on inside him. Andrew couldn't remember when he had had a greater orgasm, and he hadn't even had sex, he had rubbed a student's leg.

"Was all that still okay?" Andrew wondered breathlessly.

The force of his feelings was a bit shocking.

There was no hiding the fact that he had found something in himself that he hadn't suspected.

He was nobody who lived in the past, but he would remember this event for a long time.

Andrew had been looking for a woman like Regina. He didn't necessarily have fear of loss, wasn't necessarily jealous, but he was aware that he could not be sure that she wouldn't be lost to him.

Andrew thought it would be a good idea to pay her well at first and so he gave her a raise, although they hadn't agreed on a salary yet.

FEMDOM PART 2

It was agreed that he would pay the rent for her attic flat. So he transferred this sum to the company account of his father. He would simply claim that Regina always paid her rent in cash whenever his father's accountant asked him. He would certainly do that because he noticed everything. At the same time, Andrew transferred another thousand dollars to Regina's account for her work as an accountant. He had no idea how much was paid to such marginally employed people. But he had already heard something about minimum wage and the working conditions at Amazon, which had led to protests.

He wanted Regina to be happy. A thousand dollars plus the rent didn't seem too much to him either. After all, she had helped him to proceed with more verve, and the customers he had achieved; they brought him so much turnover that he easily boom into profits. So in his eyes, it was a good investment.

After the business was done, Andrew reviewed their last meeting.

Especially the make-up! He hadn't thought about his submissive role yet, had always seen himself as a normal and potent man, who perhaps had a not quite common but not totally unusual inclination. And then Regina came with her make-up, with lipstick, rouge, and eyeliner, and humiliated him by making him a woman. If there was a limit, it was this.

Andrew wasn't a faggot, he wasn't a drag queen!

That make-up was one thing that was taboo for him.

FEMDOM PART 2

Period.

And yet it had turned him on that Regina didn't care that she had made him up, even though he didn't want her to.

Andrew didn't want to see the pictures Regina had taken. He imagined that he came across as this poster that the gay movement had circulated in Russia.

He could imagine how much any macho man must have hated some gay poster. He had to understand it as an attack on his manhood.

Under no circumstances was anyone allowed to see these photos. Andrew would be ruined if this got out!

FEMDOM PART 2

CHAPTER 20

ON THE RUNWAY

"Caipi, caipi, caipi," it yelled in her left ear.

"Pee-pee, pee-pee!" in her right.

It was Friday. The Girls' night and Regina's first canteen party.

Brazil was the theme and while Michelle wanted to order Caipirinha, Laura urgently had to go to the toilet first.

And now it was time to enjoy student life. So far it had all been rather intimidating. What one expected from young students like Regina was already a lot. It all seemed complicated and confusing. At least Regina couldn't confirm that student life was such a great thing.

But now everything was different! The three were on the slope.

The basses boomed, the disco ball she regularly stroked with her light beams.

The feet were light and fluttered across the dance floor. Regina wore her new killer pumps. They were damn high heels, but she looked damn great in them.

Music of the nineties. They sang their hearts out, and luckily the music was loud enough that nobody had to hear it.

Pee-pee was not, Caipi was.

The next round was dragged in.

There was nothing but the party.

Eventually, there weren't three of them, there were six of them.

There were these three guys. Regina didn't know where they came from; she also didn't know their names. At some point, they were just there.

A little blond guy, Luke, had his hand in the little curve of Michelle's back; a bit too close to her bottom maybe. Laura had her lips practically in the ears of this tall Latin lover, Mandrake. She yelled something in his ear and he nodded and laughed. Regina didn't believe that he really understood what she said. The music was just too loud. But maybe it was not so important what Laura said, maybe it was more important that she blew into his ear.

Next to Regina stood Terry. He studied philosophy or English language and literature. She had already forgotten it again. He didn't answer as fast as the little blond; he didn't have a certain something. But he tried to take care of Regina. She would have rather taken the little blond one, but Terry the philosopher was now the one left for Regina. But she was also more like dancing and alcohol than guys. She didn't feel like flirting, although she found it somehow nice how much he cared for her.

Regina went to the dance floor. Michelle and Luke were already kissing in a corner, and the blonde man's hand was now kneading her bottom quite obtrusively and slipping even deeper. Laura and her Latin lover took turns yelling in each other's ears. They were so close that Laura's breasts pressed against the guy's muscular body. The light of the disco ball illuminated Laura's tongue for a moment, which she sank into the ear of her opposite. He laughed. The next moment he turned to her and bit her earlobe.

Regina imagined that he was a clever pickpocket who wanted to steal her earring with his lips and tongue.

Regina went onto the dance floor, threw her arms in the air, closed her eyes, and forgot herself.

Only when the music slowed down and got worse did she notice that she had left Terry standing. She shrugged her shoulders. It hadn't been nice, but he had certainly understood that she didn't feel like it. But when she did a pirouette, she saw him dancing a little awkwardly next to her. He smiled at her and nodded at her as if to show that the music was good. But she wasn't anymore. Regina turned her back to him and danced for herself. Terry would understand it one day.

FEMDOM PART 2

Regina forgot him and gave herself to the music. When she closed her eyes, Terry the philosophical Englishman disappeared quickly.

When Regina came back to her table the two couples tried to communicate with each other. Regina didn't take part. Finally, Laura shouted in her ear that they wanted to leave. They all wanted to go to the blonde man together.

Regina didn't like the idea very much. Not because she didn't like Terry. She had not given him a real chance. If she talked to him, he could perhaps present himself as an interesting guy. But she didn't want to find out. She didn't need a one-night stand, and she didn't need a relationship. She already had Andrew sitting at home, taking up all her time. She didn't need anybody else.

Regina imagined that she had someone at home who she could do whatever she wanted. She didn't have to be considerate. She didn't have to steal out of the room the next morning or have an unpleasant goodbye. She didn't have to pretend with a guy or herself.

Despite her alcohol level, this attitude surprised her.

And if Regina needed another reason not to join the group, it was the fact that her feet in the pumps were killing her by now. She imagined that her feet had mutated into raw meatballs. She had the best will in the world not to show them to anyone; especially not the Terry philosopher.

FEMDOM PART 2

Regina didn't want any discussions and therefore she shouted in Laura's ear that she still had something to do and would come later.

When her two friends left with their conquests, Terry stayed with her silently and expectantly.

Regina still exhaled her Caipirinha and, to be on the safe side, Terry's Caipirinha as well, so that it would go faster.

She let him know that she had to go to the toilet, but sneaked out of the disco and jumped into a taxi. For a spontaneous idea, this was a great thing as she thought. Even if it was perhaps a bit fucked up.

The taxi driver was a young, sympathetic Turk. And Regina, who was glad that she had got out of the affair so cleverly, told him about her evening and her life. At the moment, she was in a better mood and so she made the man stop at a petrol station where she got a few cans of Heineken. She offered the cab driver a can, but the driver objected saying that he was on his driving schedule and drunk driving with a customer could get her into trouble. Regina made him drive around the block three more times because she wasn't finished with her story. Finally, her story ended with her telling about Andrew. Only vaguely, of course, she didn't name names, just referred to him as an older man.

The Turkish driver couldn't believe it and they both laughed about Andrew, about everything she did with him.

FEMDOM PART 2

She gave the driver a big tip, waved after him, drank another Heineken, and then staggered into the house.

The stairs seemed to have become more as if they had moved in a few more floors since Regina had left the house in the early evening.

And since she still had her second Heineken and Andrew's apartment was nicer than her own and, above all, one floor lower, she decided to make a flying visit to him.

FEMDOM PART 2

Chapter 21

Night Watch

Andrew jumped out of his thoughts.

First, the doorbell rang, then, a few moments later, there was a banging at his apartment door.

A quick glance at his watch told him that it was three o'clock in the morning, and Andrew knelt naked in his storage room, which he hadn't cleared out this time. He knelt there and imagined Regina standing in front of him in her thin dress that accentuated her legs so beautifully. He imagined how she gave him orders, how she laughed at him, and how she forced him to do things he did not want to do.

"Hey! Open up!" it shouted through the door.

Andrew was in a mixture of panic and anger.

Regina shouted the whole house awake. She was obviously drunk.

If she said something wrong now, all his neighbors would know about the kink thing between them. But at the same time, he felt caught, after all, he was cowering naked in the storeroom and now Regina's ban on fooling around came back to his mind. He hadn't taken it too seriously so far, even though she had obviously gotten onto his trail. "How was she supposed to find out what I was doing in my spare time and if I was honest, I also found it a bit extreme that she thought she had to interfere so far in my life." Andrew wondered cluelessly. They might have to talk about that too, but not at this moment. In this moment he only felt caught.

Andrew stumbled out of the storeroom, slammed the door behind him, and shouted in the direction of the closed door, "Just a minute, I'm coming!"

Then he stormed into his bedroom, put on his jeans, he didn't have time for the shorts, and a T-shirt that already smelled a bit like sweat. As he pulled up his zipper, he tucked in his best piece. Andrew cursed and ran to the door.

When he opened the door, Regina fell towards him. He caught her before she hit the floor and he smelled the alcohol on her breath.

"It was about time, my little slave," Regina laughed, but when she screamed out the last word, he had already closed the door behind her again.

"That took a long time!" Regina was fairly intoxicated.

"Sorry, I was already in bed," Andrew replied.

"I saw your light from downstairs." Regina asserted.

FEMDOM PART 2

"I must have forgotten to turn it off," Andrew argued.

"And why are you wearing clothes? Don't you have pajamas or something? Do you sleep in jeans?" Regina asked huskily.

"I threw something on quickly. I didn't know it was you. It could have been anyone!" Andrew argued.

"You mean a client? A client, maybe? Do they still come around at night like that?" Regina laughed dirtily, but it sounded a bit like the grunt of a pig.

Andrew followed her as she staggered to the couch in his living room and fell on it.

Discreetly and without Regina noticing, he turned off the light in the storage room.

"Where is my little slave?" cried Regina.

"Here I am! What can I do for you?" Andrew asked courteously.

"That's right! You can do something for me! Tonight you'll do something for me! So far, all I've ever done for you is enjoying the pleasure. Now it's my turn!" Regina babbled in her drowsiness.

"How can I help you?" asked Andrew, but there was no humility in his voice. Rather, he was angry.

"First, I want a drink. A whiskey! On the rocks. And then you can massage my feet! They really fucking hurt my feet.

FEMDOM PART 2

Shit hurts," Regina repeated. Regina tried to take off her pumps, but she didn't get far, then she hissed with pain, "Ow, ow, ow! Come here, slave, and take off my shoes! You may caress my divine feet!" She laughed.

Andrew knelt in front of her and slowly pulled the pumps from her foot, but not without some reproaches.

"Careful, damn it, you gross motorist!" Regina scolded.

She laughed.

"Rub my feet! Come on! It'll make you horny!" Regina demanded.

She laughed cackling again.

"You can lick them clean! And maybe I'll let you lick something else afterward!" Regina stated playfully.

"May I suggest something better?" Andrew didn't wait for her permission but immediately went on, "How about a nice, warm foot bath. How's that?" He didn't feel like playing games when she was in that condition.

"Very good! Very good. I hereby give you the order to bathe my feet! Like Cleopatra. And I want fried eggs. Yes, slave. That's how you end a bender. With nice fried eggs! I hope you have eggs." Regina yelled in her drunken state.

Before Andrew could answer, she added: "I mean in the fridge! You know what I mean?"

FEMDOM PART 2

He didn't even nod. He just said, "I'll go prepare the water!"

So he left the living room and filled a tub with hot water and some bath salts.

Andrew ignored the request for the whiskey. But when he came back with the bowl and a towel, she had already opened her last Heineken and half-empty it.

Andrew knelt in front of her, took her feet, let them glide slowly into the warm water, and then massaged her gently. He had never done this before, but he remembered the conversation about foot massages between John Travolta and Samuel L. Jackson in Pulp Fiction. Someone in the conversation suggested that foot massages were a sign of manhood. So Andrew could live with being in this group. He also had something of John Travolta, he thought.

"Oh, that's good!" purred Regina. "You are the best sex slave one could wish for! I think I'll let you massage something else completely different," Regina laughed again and babbled for a while. But Andrew noticed that her voice became quieter and more and more incomprehensible. The warm water and the alcohol obviously tired her.

Once she belched loudly and then stammered, "Oh God, I almost puked all over your apartment!"

But Regina soon recovered from her fatigue. She babbled, demanded fried eggs from him again, because that's the way you eat them, after a long night, she babbled something else, and then at some point, she was very quiet.

FEMDOM PART 2

When Andrew looked up, she had dozed off. Regina's mouth was open and slowly a saliva thread ran out of the corner of her mouth.

Andrew carefully lifted her feet out of the bath, dried them, and took the beer can out of her hands.

From his bedroom, Andrew took a blanket and put it over Regina.

Andrew had never done such a thing before. To take care of a woman like that. In his circle, the style was always important. One didn't get drunk indiscriminately and didn't let oneself go like that. His mother had instilled it into him. More or less nouveau riche as she was, she had placed a lot of value on the appropriate appearance of the family and that was also communicated to Andrew. And he had always believed in it. He had already got drunk, also unrestrainedly, but never in the presence of a girlfriend, but at best with his drinking buddies and never in the city, always on vacations. He thought there was a difference.

Andrew had even taken pleasure in helping Regina. Even something he had not thought possible. In his world, people bought services like maids or cooks or... others.

Andrew found himself quite advanced in his development towards being a different person. This whole thing between them was obviously not just sexual. It also changed him for the better. He made more sales, put in more effort, massaged women's feet, and wiped away saliva threads.

FEMDOM PART 2

Andrew considered whether he should go to his own bed, whether he should perhaps carry Regina up to her bed, but he decided against it. Instead, he pushed an armchair into place and sat down beside her for a night watch.

When Regina woke up the next morning, she should calmly know that Andrew had watched her throughout the night.

But it took him a while to fall asleep because the alcohol made Regina snore quite loudly and annoyingly.

Dominas were not perfect either.

CHAPTER 22

IF YOU WERE SATISFIED

The sunrays pricked Regina's eyes like long rusty needles.

Where was she?

Regina remembered that she had moved and she wasn't in her old nursery. But she also didn't lie in the bed in her new apartment. What was covering her was not her flowered plumage.

"Terry the Philosopher! Wasn't I sleeping with him? Was I in his bed, was he next to me? Did I have to get out of bed quietly? Find my clothes and then disappear silently? Shit." Regina wondered. But that would be the only way, because she didn't even remember fucking him, and she definitely didn't want to see him.

"Oh, God!" Regina sighed.

She now remembered a Turkish cab driver and Heineken at the gas station, and then a lot of stairs. "Could I have even had the cabbie?" Regina wondered cluelessly.

Regina moaned.

FEMDOM PART 2

Her head was heavy, her throat dry, her tongue covered. She moved and noticed that she was tense. She didn't lie in a bed, but on a couch.

Regina closed her eyes.

She didn't need this at all.

She didn't want to tiptoe around a strange flat to find her clothes.

But if she had to get up, then she must do immediately.

Now, while Regina still had time to escape unnoticed.

She moaned, rubbed her eyes, and had to realize that the apartment looked quite familiar to her. It was Andrew's, and before she panicked if she had done things she regretted, she realized that she still had her clothes on. And she didn't necessarily smell nice, but sweaty and like cold cigarette smoke.

Well, it was still better than being naked in a strange bed.

Regina straightened up, but unfortunately too fast so that the headache came back again.

"Oh, Madame is awake too!" A voice mocked her.

Regina got a fright and Andrew's voice rattled in her head. He had just come out of the kitchen and stood there with a grin that was so wide that she could get sick.

"What time is it?" she murmured.

FEMDOM PART 2

"10:30," Andrew replied.

"10:30?" Regina was shocked.

"Ten thirty." Andrew asserted.

"Shit!" Regina breathed.

"Don't worry, it's Saturday at ten thirty! You're not missing much." Andrew joked.

"Very funny!" Regina smirked.

"Better not ask how you're feeling." Andrew teased.

"I'd better not." Regina was feeling heavy-headed.

"How do your feet feel?" Andrew asked.

"My feet?" Regina asked in sheer surprise.

"Today you're gonna ask all those questions." Andrew teased again.

"Sorry. But what about my feet?" Regina tried to recall something.

"You came all the way over to my house last night to get a foot massage," Andrew replied.

"So?" Regina demanded.

"So, I want to know if I did a good job." Andrew chuckled.

FEMDOM PART 2

Regina leaned back on the couch, tried to concentrate on her feet, but her feet didn't let on that they felt somehow better than the rest of her body.

"I feel nothing special!" Regina replied.

Andrew appeared seriously disappointed.

"So I came over to your place last night?" Regina asked curiously.

"Exactly," Andrew replied.

"And I wanted a foot massage." Regina tried to recall her last night's adventure.

"And a whiskey. And fried eggs. But they weren't available yesterday. You can have them today if you want. Shall we start with the whiskey?" Andrew teased.

"Please don't. It makes me puke." Regina breathed.

"By the way, you almost did yesterday," Andrew smirked.

"Vomited?" Regina was shocked and embarrassed.

"Yes, my lady! I put another bucket next to the couch for your safety. Anything for my mistress!" Andrew teased.

"Can you stop that?" Regina seemed overly embarrassed.

"Stop what?" Andrew teased back.

"The dominatrix bullshit. I don't feel like it." Regina admonished.

FEMDOM PART 2

"No problem. How about those fried eggs for breakfast? I already got rolls and orange juice. I got some bacon, too." Andrew proposed.

Regina couldn't make up her mind.

"Can I bring you a pencil and paper?" Andrew proposed teasingly.

"What for?" Regina was awestruck.

"Then you can make a list of pros and cons." Andrew chuckled.

"I don't feel like joking!" Regina admonished.

"Then let me make the decision for you. You're gonna go upstairs and take a nice long shower with lots of shower lotion, put on some serious deodorant, put on something fresh if you like, the comfortable baggy pants and the cuddly sweatshirt for Sundays, and then you're gonna come downstairs without any dominatrix affectations where you'll find a freshly laundered breakfast of hangovers." Andrew proposed courteously.

"Like me then, you mean?" Regina smelled her clothes.

"I see your mind is slowly returning." Andrew joked.

Regina replied, "Okay, but you have to answer me one more question, otherwise I'll get knocked out in the shower. Did I embarrass myself badly yesterday?"

"You were charming like a little lady." Andrew teased.

FEMDOM PART 2

"I can fool myself." Regina rebuffed.

"But it's more fun when I do it for you like I'm your slave. Your sex slave, to be exact." Andrew remarked playfully.

"Oh God, is that what I called you? Sex slave? How embarrassing!" Regina felt her cheeks burning with embarrassment.

"I thought it was funny!" Andrew replied.

"I can imagine. Did I say anything else?" Regina inquired.

"You promised me all kinds of sexual services. But since you didn't write them down, they're now lost forever, and I have to keep hoping." Andrew teased.

"But other than that, I haven't made too much of a fool of myself?" Regina seemed helpless.

"It all stayed within reason," Andrew remarked.

"All right." Regina sighed.

Regina got up laboriously, rubbed her neck, and sighed, "Next time you won't let me sleep on the couch!"

"I am sorry, but then you must give me the instructions beforehand. You didn't leave me an alcohol coma will!" Andrew teased.

"That's okay!" Regina replied.

FEMDOM PART 2

When she got up, her brain was banging against the top of her skull again. She got up, staggering.

"You want me to carry you up?" Andrew proposed.

"You keep your hands off me!" Regina seemed defiant.

"Very well, madam," Andrew smirked.

"I can still do it alone! And the fried eggs better be great!" Regina stated.

"Then what?" Andrew inquired.

"Then I'll whip my little sex slave's skin into fine strips!" Regina admonished.

"Sounds like you're feeling better already!" Andrew remarked playfully.

Regina tried to scrape together as much dignity as she could. She raised her head, tried to walk upright and straight, and to make a reasonably respectable exit. So she stalked barefoot past him, up the stairs to her apartment.

She undressed on the way to the shower, dropped her clothes on the floor behind her at random. Maybe she let Andrew pick them up later. He seemed to want to distinguish himself as a houseman and servant.

As the water of the shower glided over her body and slowly got her circulation going, Regina sighed stretched out. She stood in the shower for a long time. Very long. When she finally got out, her fingertips were already shriveled, her

FEMDOM PART 2

headache was still there, but it had become a little duller. In front of her wardrobe, she was thinking about how she should dress for breakfast with Andrew. But she decided, as he had suggested, on the baggy sweatpants and an equally baggy hoodie. With her hair still wet and her hood up, Regina went back downstairs and rang the bell.

A moment later Andrew opened it too.

"You look better!" He appreciated.

"Thank you. My headache hasn't gone away." Regina complained.

"I have some pills." Andrew offered.

He led Regina into the kitchen, where she sat down at the table. It was just set for her.

He made her a coffee with his coffee maker of considerable size, which he served her immediately.

Regina took a roll from the basket.

"Do you have any Nutella?" Regina inquired.

"Sorry, I don't. But tomorrow." Andrew replied.

"No problem," Regina replied back.

She made a cheese sandwich instead and ate it while Andrew fried two eggs and bacon for her. She enjoyed breakfast in silence and he was equally at peace.

FEMDOM PART 2

When the eggs were ready, he served them to her and then stood beside the table like a servant. He had even draped the kitchen towel over her forearm.

"Aren't you hungry?" she asked.

"I've already had breakfast," Andrew said.

"Sit down anyway. I can't have it with you standing there!" Regina remarked.

"Suit yourself," Andrew replied.

He sat down. Regina chewed for a while, and then she said irritably, "Have a coffee or a juice! It annoys me when you hang around like that! We aren't playing games right now!"

"Okay." Andrew obeyed.

Andrew got up and made himself a coffee with the machine that made loud coffee and all kinds of noises. Finally, he sat back down at the table.

"We really have to set some rules at some point, how this is supposed to work between us," Regina said.

"We really should," Andrew replied.

"I mean, you don't have to play the submissive here. I didn't behave like the Lady or the Madame or the Countess and what not. I don't even remember what I said. You don't have to be a slave today." Regina was somewhat agitated.

FEMDOM PART 2

"Okay." Andrew tried to calm down the temperament.

"Okay? Is that all? I'd rather you said something. My brain is still in intensive care." Regina yelled irately.

"But do you really wanna do this now? Without preparation?" Andrew asked.

"Of course not! What are you thinking?" Regina was curious.

"Let me guess, you're just making a list." Andrew teased.

"Exactly. You can laugh at this, but lists have served me well so far. When I plan things, they usually go according to plan. If I had planned better yesterday, I wouldn't have come to your house drunk, I wouldn't have slept on your couch, and I would have said all kinds of things I shouldn't have said, and which I'm sure you remember pretty well, but I don't remember them at all." Regina replied annoyingly.

"Maybe you're right." Andrew asserted.

"I don't believe that yesterday I was consolidating my authority!" Regina remarked.

"But maybe that wasn't what it was all about," Andrew stated.

"About authority? I thought it was about nothing else. Isn't that what you want? My authority?" Regina yelped.

"But maybe not always and not exclusively. It's not what it's all about right now." Andrew smiled.

"You're right. We need to professionalize our relationship a bit." Regina proposed.

Andrew noted that she used the word "relationship". He was aware, of course, that she had probably used it in a businesslike, not a romantic, way.

****

Regina cut herself a piece of her fried egg. The egg yolk ran off. She gulped it with a piece of her bread roll.

"But one thing is important to me", said Andrew. "This. All this must remain between us. No one must know about it. Not your friends, not even your best. No one. No matter how far away the person is. And if he's on a mission to Mars and there's no fuel to get back. No one can know about it! Okay?" Andrew seemed serious.

Regina looked at him. She was astonished that he took such a serious tone. But she could understand him. She didn't like to be known as a dominatrix either. Even if she was not one.

Against this background, she became painfully aware that she had been quite generous with all kinds of information the previous evening. She remembered now vaguely the taxi driver. She remembered that he had such nice dimples and she remembered that she had asked him if his girlfriend was a dental assistant because his teeth were so straight, so white and so flawless. "Was that actually racist? So what, I didn't think the Turkish taxi driver had a friend with higher education? Or was I racist towards dental assistants right now?" Regina didn't know.

But she remembered the name of the taxi driver. Emin perhaps. And from the shreds of her memory, she constructed that she had babbled about this philosopher Terry and about a guy whose dominatrix she was. Or something like that. But maybe she just imagined the last thing. She couldn't remember if she hadn't offered the taxi driver to make him her slave. But since Andrew remembered the term "sex slave", she guessed it hadn't gone to the taxi driver.

"What about Michelle and Laura? Had I told them about that too?" Regina didn't know. But she couldn't really imagine it. And the taxi driver was probably used to strange people telling him strange stories. He had probably driven a dozen dominatrices around town the previous day alone. There was one more or less certainly not something he told the world about. But no matter how much she told herself all kinds of things, it was all super embarrassing for her!

Anyway, Regina had learned her lesson.

She had a bad conscience because of her loose mouth, but she didn't feel called to confession. So her conclusion was, "Okay. Not a word to anyone. But that goes for both of us!"

Andrew nodded. "That goes without saying!"

"Well, let's talk. I have to make my list first." Regina remarked.

"I know. How was your evening?" Andrew asked.

Regina sighed and thought, "Obviously too much alcohol. Otherwise, it was nice. Let off steam. Girls' night out. That kind of thing."

Regina told Andrew about the party. She talked about the pre-glazing, the three guys who showed up last night. She told about Terry, with whom she didn't want to get involved. But instead of saying that she had enough to do with Andrew and therefore didn't feel like having another guy, she remained vague on this point. Regina thought that it was a bit early to admit any emotional connection with Andrew. Not before they had clarified the status of their relationship. When she was thinking this thought in her brain, she also realized that she used the term "relationship". Like Andrew, she didn't know much about it yet, so she left it at that.

So while Regina was having breakfast and talking, Michelle and Laura messaged her in her WhatsApp. They both wanted to know where she was, why she had disappeared the night before. Both accused her of everything she had missed.

Both had probably ended up in the box with their respective guy.

Regina didn't think she had missed much. But she didn't want to write the truth either. She had just made a pact to keep the truth to herself. So she talked herself out of it by saying she had drunk too much and felt sick. That wasn't really wrong, was it? Either she couldn't take as much as Michelle and Laura or she'd really been drinking a lot more. Anyway, Regina wondered how they could still go to bed with guys.

Maybe she really wasn't used to it. Maybe she was just getting too old for it. She was about three years older than the girls. She looked at Andrew, who was another ten years older than her. He didn't look like he was going to be drinking much either.

If Regina thought about her head, then maybe it wasn't a bad decision. Anyway, she had enough of alcohol for the time being.

The messages that came in on her smartphone reported that Terry had asked for her. But Regina forbade Michelle and Laura to give out her number. She had to think it all over first. But generally, her attitude hadn't changed. Andrew had taken care of her in an exemplary way. That didn't make him more than what he was now, but it was nice how he poured coffee over her, how he brought her headache pills and a glass of water, how he cleared the table while she talked. Andrew asked questions, was interested in her and Regina had the feeling that she didn't have to do anything in return. She could just enjoy it.

Regina considered if she had to throw him some dominant bone so he could have some fun too, but she didn't feel like improvising anything. Here in his kitchen so early in the morning was just not the right moment.

Chapter 23

Seductive Preparation

Regina had overcome her hangover in the meantime. Her body was well again; her ego was not yet so sure that it hadn't got some dents. She thought that she hadn't acted with grace and dignity the night before.

But Andrew had been courteous. The chemistry between them was just right.

He had behaved like a gentleman and she wanted to reward him for that.

But for now, she turned over her pad and started a new page. The next session was on! It was much more exciting to plan than to find out the status of their "relationship".

First, she thought about a structure, and then she drew a few lines with a ruler.

On the left, Regina wanted to sketch the course of her next meeting. On the right side, there was a category at the top, where she entered the utensils she had herself. Below that there was one she could buy in the supermarket and below that there was another category with the sex toys she had bought in the online sex shop.

In this column were handcuffs and leg irons, a face mask, and a ball gag. She had googled the name but knew the part from some porn movies she had watched for study purposes.

Regina had become quite an expert with these toys in a short period of time, although she hadn't used one yet. Her research on the Internet had shown that these things were all more complicated than she had thought. For example, she had thought that silk scarves would be a good idea to tie Andrew up. Silk is soft, delicate, so it should be perfect. But Regina had quickly found out that silk was very bad for bondage because the fibers were so thin that knots were very difficult to untie. She had to be careful with ropes because they cut into the skin. There was a lot to know about bondage alone. It all had more to do with safety and responsibility than she had thought.

Regina actually only wanted to tie Andrew to the bed. But this whole Sado-Masochism scene on the internet put an amazing amount of emphasis on security. And that wasn't necessarily wrong. One heard again and again about the fire brigade, which had to come to cut handcuffs because the keys had been lost during love play. Regina wanted to avoid that by all means.

She ordered these things with Andrew's credit card. He should pay for it! He was the beneficiary after all.

FEMDOM PART 2

And while Regina was wondering about the financials, she had found a ridiculously high amount on her account, which Andrew had transferred to her.

"You can't just transfer over a thousand Euros like that!" she had reproached him.

"Why not? It is my money! I can do what I want with it. It comes from my bank account." Andrew countered.

"I'm not registered as your employee," Regina argued.

"So what? You don't work for me like that. You work for me in a different way." Andrew replied.

"Explain that to the IRS when such sums are regularly transferred from your account to mine!" Regina was furious.

"Then I'll just hire you. You'll be my full-time accountant!" Andrew stated.

"I don't do that much for you!" Regina admonished.

"I think you do an awful lot for me. I'm very happy." Andrew countered.

"I don't want to get paid for it. At least not like this." Regina stated sternly.

"Why not? You do something for me, and that's what I pay you for. You made me take on a lot of jobs. I'm working a lot more than I did a month ago. I have more clients, I have more assignments, and I make more money!" Andrew explained.

"I'm moonlighting," Regina argued irately.

"I'm paying you to do the books. Do your job and make yourself legal!" Andrew argued.

Regina was speechless because of Andrew's naivety. "How could anyone be so narrow-minded? He had not the slightest idea of the simplest business connections." Regina wondered inwardly.

"It is not that simple. You'd have to hire me for real." Regina remarked.

"Then I'll hire you right. Full-time and everything!" Andrew proposed.

"Do you know how expensive that is?" Regina inquired.

"I don't think you know how much you cost me," Andrew remarked heart fully.

They looked at each other for a moment. They both knew what Andrew had just intimated.

This sentence upset Regina a bit.

"Your father will not agree to such a thing. It makes perfect sense that your bookkeeping is done by your father's company. Why should you hire your own accountant full-time? Besides, I'm probably not allowed to make that much money as a student. After all, I get some support from the university for studies."

"Firstly, I'm my own boss. Secondly, my father has no say in my business!" Andrew countered sternly.

"These are two arguments. Great!" Regina commented.

"Okay, if you don't want that, then we'll do it differently. I'll take out all my cash and give it to you! Is that better? I'll tell the IRS I'm a compulsive gambler and I burn all my money in the ATM. Happy?" Andrew said jokingly somehow.

Regina mumbled. "It wasn't only about the way the money came to me. It was mainly about the amount. It was all just too much." She told him that too.

"Fine! Fine. Then you'll get less and in cash, and we're done. Satisfied? Can you please dominate me again?" Andrew was desperate.

Regina had to laugh. Maybe Andrew was right.

She dropped the subject, even though they hadn't agreed on a sum.

So Regina kept on working on her list and when she was finished she had filled the page and planned her next session with Andrew. It worked. There was so much potential in her, it was amazing what talents you could discover!

FEMDOM PART 2

CHAPTER 24

THE FATHERFUL TORTURE BENCH

"Drop your clothes! Keep your shorts on." Regina commanded.

Regina stood in his flat. She liked to stand in front of Andrew with her legs apart. She enjoyed his attention and how obedient he was. He immediately became a few centimeters shorter when he heard the order. She saw him swallow. It was wonderful how fast it went! Perhaps, she even saw him trembling at her burning dominance.

Andrew was coy, playing with the top button on his shirt, nibbling on it as if he was embarrassed. Regina felt as if he was doing a striptease for her. Only without dancing, without sweeping movements. But she could tell that Andrew was very aware of his movements. Very slowly he opened one button after the other. Regina's eyes captured his gaze as if she was holding him on an invisible leash.

It seemed to her as if she could see directly into his soul as if he opened himself to her. Andrew took off his shirt and stood still for a moment. She used the moment to look at his naked upper body. She thought that women had a more beautiful upper body than men. Very few men were handsome in her eyes. Andrew had a tiny attachment of the abdomen, but also some pectoral muscles. He was not a bodybuilder, but it was still okay. Beautiful was something else, but Regina wasn't concerned with appearances. After all, she wasn't exactly a supermodel either.

Andrew fiddled with his belt but Regina slowed him down, "First the shoes and the socks!" and then she added a basic rule, "Here's a basic rule. I never want to see you in socks. If you take anything off, always put off the socks before the trousers. Got it?"

Andrew nodded obediently.

"Good!! Naked man's legs in socks look so stupid!" Regina reacted.

Andrew nodded, bent over, and took off his shoes first, then his socks.

Regina was satisfied. She could wish for such a thing and he kept to it. She imagined that she could drive all the quirks out of him and make him a perfect, obedient companion. How great was that? She could do anything with him! Still, maybe they could be equal from time to time and have fun together above the waist.

Andrew put his shoes next to each other, straightened up again and waited for another command.

"What are you waiting for? You know what you have to do," Regina yapped at him and caught his gaze as he unbuckled his belt. Regina directed him with the slightest movement of her eyes.

Andrew pulled down his trousers and slipped out of them.

"And now into the bedroom!" Regina commanded.

He looked at her. He hadn't expected this. She thought it was cute how easy he was to see through him.

"On the bed," Regina ordered.

Andrew obeyed.

Regina put down the bag, unzipped the zipper, and first, she put the blindfold on him.

One last time he looked at her. She recognized concern in his eyes and next to it this infinite horniness. Then it became black around him.

She took his left arm and put one of the handcuffs she had just bought first on him. They were the expensive ones. Regina smelled the spicy smell of the leather. Andrew let it happen, even as she fastened his arm to the bedpost. She actually wanted to get up and sit on the edge of the bed on the other side, but then she became brave, climbed onto the bed, and sat on his bare chest while she fixed his second arm to the other bedpost. As she fixed his arm, she bent forward so that her freshly washed hair brushed across his face. It might look as if this movement was a coincidence, but it was calculated. Regina could imagine what the level of intoxication the smell of her hair must have done to his nose.

When both his arms were tied, Regina took the opportunity to have a close look at Andrew. She had never been so close to him before. She formed her hands into claws and scratched over his chest like a predatory caste.

Andrew flinched and sucked in the air sharply. She twisted his long erect nipples.

Regina felt the feeling of her power. It was like a drug, she was intoxicated.

Regina leaned over him. Again her hair stroked over him, over his breast, then over his cheeks. She felt how the tiny touches of her hairs on his chest excited him, that his nerves went crazy as if they had received small electric shocks. She looked at the red streaks her nails had drawn on his chest.

"The marks I will leave on your soul will not disappear as quickly as the scratches here!" Regina whispered into his ear.

She scratched his chest again, but now she squeezed harder and caused Andrew severe pain.

"But the pain I will inflict on your soul will be much more intense than the pain on your skin." Regina teased seductively.

Andrew nodded and wanted to say something but Regina put her index finger on his lips. His heartfelt it was struck by a thunderbolt and was beating like a thousand drums.

"You say nothing. I want to hear nothing from you but a confession! Understood?" Regina asked appealingly.

Andrew nodded although he had no idea what he should confess. He could feel his mind getting hypnotized by her seductive voice.

"Very well. You'll see what I'm getting at!" Regina teased seductively.

Andrew lay still and she took her index finger from his lips.

Then Regina turned around on his chest and chained his legs to the posts at the foot end.

She got down from him and watched her work, then she bent down to him and breathed into his ear, "Now you are totally at my mercy!"

Andrew's chest rose and fell heavily, and under his shorts, the tent was about to burst. At least, that's what she thought. She could even see a faint stain on the crotch, "He had been leaking just at my mere teases."

Regina went through her bag and found what she was looking for.

But before she did anything, she stood very still for a while, not moving.

FEMDOM PART 2

Since Andrew couldn't see anything anymore, he only had his ears to hear what was going on around him. But if there was nothing more to hear because she didn't make a sound, then there was nothing more than his imagination, which surely had to drive him mad!

She smiled and looked at him as he turned his head to hear something. He lay there before her like an expensive buffet at a wedding. Or like a sacrifice on the altar. She couldn't make up her mind. She liked both pictures.

Finally, Regina moved. Slowly, very slowly.

****

Andrew didn't know what happened to him. He had never experienced anything like it. Was there anything greater than what just happened? He didn't know what it was, but he knew he wouldn't forget this so quickly. And he didn't even know what to expect. He was already sorry that this would be over one day, and it hadn't even really started yet!

It was quiet. So quiet. Andrew turned his head.

Was Regina still there? Had she gone away? His agitated mind kept on guessing.

But then Andrew should have heard her steps. He didn't know. But Regina was obviously not there anymore. Why else would she keep so quiet? His muscles tightened up like he was expecting a nasty surprise.

FEMDOM PART 2

A blow, maybe. His restless mind screamed into his aroused mind.

But nothing came.

Thrown back on himself, Andrew could hear the rush of his blood in his ears. He felt his chest rise and fall, and he tugged at his shackles once. But it just rattled a little metallically.

His bed had been expensive. He knew that no matter how hard he tugged, he couldn't break free. He was just too quality-conscious in his buying decisions! The bed frame, for example, was made of hand-welded steel frames by a Finnish designer. He was considered the shooting star in the scene and it was said that the originals could one day be worth as much as the Barcelona armchairs by Mies van der Rohe! The fact that a Finnish designer dealt with steel instead of wood was already considered revolutionary. Not many people were aware that design goods like art could become enormously valuable. So it wasn't throwing money out the window to spend large four-figure sums on "simple" beds. It was an investment. And Andrew slept on it! Unfortunately few people shared his enthusiasm, his father, for example, didn't.

But all this was then only a fleeting thought because Andrew was still trapped!

His heart was beating violently in his chest. And then finally a sound!

FEMDOM PART 2

A small crack, as if a wooden stick had been broken through.

In the next moment, the impressions shot up at him.

A rubbing sound, then a hissing sound right at his ear, and the smell of sulfur rose to his nose.

Regina had lit a match.

Andrew felt the heat on his cheek. It wasn't hot, but his heart was beating faster now. She wasn't only playing with him, she was playing with fire!

The fear rose up in Andrew.

He trusted her.

He didn't think she'd burn him in his own bed. She wasn't one of those. Regina was a little square who was totally normal and already thought he was a pervert because he liked strong women. She made lists. That said it all!

She put something under his nose. The soapy smell of a candle went up to his nose, and then he smelled the candle being lit. He could even hear the wick crackle softly as it caught fire.

Then a breeze and the stench of burning wood entered his nose. Regina had waved the match.

Then there was silence again.

FEMDOM PART 2

The smell hung in the air for a while, especially the sulfur from the match. But there was nothing else to hear or smell.

The waiting tore at his nerves, but it was just as cool to wait for what would happen next.

It was madness! It was intense anticipation! It was an indescribable arousal! Or perhaps, a blend of all these strong, overwhelming emotions.

And then Andrew jumped up.

Something splashed on his chest. A liquid. It took him a split second to understand what it was. It was liquid wax, and it solidified almost instantly on his skin.

A slight pain passed through him, but it was bearable. The wax dripped first on his left nipple, then on his right nipple, then across his chest. It suddenly became hotter, but not unbearable, then a little cooler again. Sometimes it just dripped, and then it ran like a small stream.

Now it dripped into his navel, and it continued to flow until his whole navel was filled with wax.

It felt strange on his skin because when the wax dried, it seemed to contract. Where he had been hit, his skin was burning.

Nothing happened again for a while, and then Andrew suddenly felt something sharp on his skin, very close to his left nipple. It was one of Regina's fingernails, which playfully ran across his chest, went under the encrusted wax layer, and peeled it off his skin. Andrew felt a slight pull, and then coolness, as the heat of the wax disappeared from his skin. Slowly, her finger kept on touching and lifting the dried wax from his chest. Sometimes it pulled when one of the few hairs on his chest was torn out.

But Regina didn't care about it.

She played with his body; made him her object and Andrew could do nothing but bear it. But he didn't bear it, he enjoyed it. It was an unbelievable feeling and he would never have thought that candle wax could be so exciting.

Eventually, she tampered with the dried pond in his navel. Regina squeezed his belly and then pulled the plug out and with it slowly, so that it became uncomfortable, some of his hair.

"Now I have an imprint of your navel," Regina said curtly, and Andrew was torn from his contemplation.

"I should throw your whole body in hot wax and make an imprint of it. What do you think?" Regina teased.

He knew he wasn't allowed to say anything, so he just shook his head.

"You're right! It's not worth it. You're not so great that you should be made into a wax figure." Regina remarked playfully.

Her cold voice contrasted with the heat on his skin, and it irritated him.

FEMDOM PART 2

"You know, I was nice. Really nice. If I hadn't been so nice, I would have used depilatory wax. And then I would have waxed your whole body. You can't imagine how it burns when all your hair is torn out of your skin in one go. With roots and all!" Regina stated seductively.

Regina was silent, and the idea sank into Andrew's mind. She could do it; he couldn't help himself after all. He couldn't imagine himself without body hair. It was just part of being a man! Young people shave everywhere nowadays, even young men. He had seen it in a documentary. But for him, it was a sign of femininity. Women had soft skin, they were depilated and soft. Men smelled of sweat and had hair on their legs!

"I have the wax here. I can heat it up very quickly. And then we'll go over your whole body, including your bikini line!" Regina teased alluringly.

She laughed coldly, and Andrew ran down her back just as cold.

"It's all a question of whether you cooperate. If you confess, you might get around it!" Regina admonished.

"What am I going to confess to?" She took it from him.

Smack!

A slap hit him out of nowhere.

It wasn't the pain, it was the surprise that made his heart race. Andrew was terrified.

FEMDOM PART 2

"You shall not speak without my permission!" Regina lorded him over, and now Andrew really got a little frightened. Because he hadn't expected this reaction.

His cheek was burning.

"Your behavior has brought you one giant step closer to a waxing cure, my slave!" Regina asserted.

Andrew was silent. He had to avoid waxing at all costs. He didn't want to be demoted to a woman again. Make-up could be wiped off again, but if she robbed him of his hair, wasn't he something like a Samson? Defenseless and helpless, robbed of his manly powers? He had to obey. He had to do what he could to keep her from becoming angrier.

"Are you gonna be good now?" Regina asked seductively.

He didn't want the wax, the treatment, or emasculation. Still, Andrew nodded. He couldn't bear the word "good," though.

"All right. We'll see!" Regina stated sternly.

She rummaged in her bag again.

"What could happen now?" Andrew wondered breathlessly.

Then there was an awkward silence again.

The excruciating waiting again.

"What was she doing?" Andrew thought cluelessly.

FEMDOM PART 2

Nothing happened.

Andrew was thrown back on himself. Again and again, his nerve endings played a trick on him, expecting something that didn't come, telling his brain a stimulus that didn't exist. Again and again, his body played a trick on him. There was nothing, but his body simply invented something, like phantom pain.

And then he was no longer so sure that there was nothing because suddenly his nerves screamed out especially loud and he thought he felt a draft. Then again nothing, then again a caress, unbelievably tender. He felt as if he had been caressed by a cobweb in the wind. The thought startled him and strong goosebumps ran down his back. "Was it really a spider?" Andrew screamed inwardly.

There it was again!

Andrew reared up against his shackles.

"Don't you like it?" Regina laughed. "It will be even better in a moment!"

The unknown touched him again. And now he recognized it, too. It was a feather. She stroked him with a feather, one of those delicate and tingling feathers!

Regina caressed all over his body, and his hypersensitive nerves calmed down because they had understood.

But now something else happened.

It tickled!

FEMDOM PART 2

It tickled very badly.

Andrew got scared and shook himself.

He couldn't defend himself, he couldn't protect himself.

It tickled insanely.

The spring attacked him on the sole of his left foot and then under his right armpit.

Andrew reared up, tugging wildly at his ankles so that the bed moved.

"Please don't! Please! No! Please don't!" he cried, he begged, he begged. But he had to laugh through all this. He didn't want to. He was serious. Bitterly serious. But he laughed.

It was unbearable.

But Regina didn't react. She said nothing, she didn't betray her position. She attacked suddenly and stroked him with this cursed feather.

He was at her mercy.

Completely.

He was helpless.

He had to laugh, at the same time he was angry.

So much was tugging at him.

FEMDOM PART 2

Andrew tried to control himself, but he couldn't.

He was in her hands.

He was completely at her mercy, and he was completely helpless.

"Please. Please. Please. Please. Please. Please. Please." He pleaded, he begged, he gritted his teeth so as not to laugh, "I'll do anything you say! But please stop!"

Regina stopped immediately.

"You shouldn't say such things. 'I'll do anything you say.' That's just unprofessional. It always ends badly." Regina admonished irately.

She didn't say anything and Andrew had a chance to calm down a bit. He was breathing heavily and beads of sweat had formed on his body.

"Please. Please. Please. "Please. Please." Andrew huffed and puffed.

"Do you realize you're talking again?" Regina asked sternly.

He expected another slap or some other punishment. But nothing happened.

"At least your horniness is gone! That's something!" Regina teased.

In fact, his erection had subsided.

FEMDOM PART 2

"Am I not so hot after all, or is it your age? Can't you take it much longer?" Regina asked seductively.

She laughed coldly.

How humiliating it was!

What was she doing with him?

Andrew tried to calm down, but it was slow.

Meanwhile, she was standing there. She didn't bother to be quiet; he could hear her move, take a few steps.

Regina seemed to be waiting.

Andrew rolled around in his bed as far as his restraints would allow. He just had to give his nerves a few dependable stimuli.

When he calmed down, she spoke again, "I have a feeling I've got your little friend pretty well in hand. Do you think I can get him up with my words alone?" She paused for a moment, and then her words cut coldly into his ear. "Show me some respect and straighten up your little dick."

Andrew could feel it starting to tingle between his legs. He couldn't fight back. He wanted to. He wanted to please and obey her, and so he felt the blood shoot into his abdomen and slowly achieve the desired effect.

Regina laughed when she saw it. "You are so easily manipulated!"

FEMDOM PART 2

Andrew would have loved to sink into his bed in shame, with the blanket over his head! He was completely at the mercy of her insults and humiliations, and he enjoyed it too.

"Good boy! Good boy, you are obedient, no one can deny it!" She laughed again seductively.

"Now I want to see how fast I can make you weak again!" Regina teased playfully.

Andrew had a bad feeling.

"You know, the feather and the candle, I had them at home. It was no problem. I had to go outside for the next part. All the way to the park." Regina stated teasingly.

Something clapped his chest at the same moment. It was a plant. He smelled the spicy smell. It wasn't unpleasant at first, and it stayed with that one touch.

"Was that it already?" Andrew thought as he huffed and puffed.

But the next moment it started to itch and burn terribly on his skin.

"I think you can guess what this is!" Regina chuckled deviously.

It was nettles!

Slowly the burning grew and became unbearable. They pricked him like a thousand tiny needles

FEMDOM PART 2

Andrew moaned. It was madness. It had to stop! He writhed in his bondage, tried to roll on his back to rub against the fabric. But he couldn't do it.

His body was at her mercy. His mind was at her mercy

"I see it's going downhill again! I'm glad you're in such good control!" Regina said wickedly.

Andrew didn't care. Yeah, Regina was right. His erection was gone again.

He was just busy with the itching on his chest.

"Please, please! Make it stop," he begged.

She laughed at him.

"Please? I'll do anything you say?" She imitated his voice teasingly...

He nodded violently.

"I won't be like that for once! I'm not a monster!" Regina rebuffed.

Then Andrew felt her hand on his chest, rubbing quickly over it, softening his pain.

"Thank you," he murmured.

She stopped immediately, and the pain was back.

"What did you say?" Regina asked sternly.

FEMDOM PART 2

He didn't know what to do. He had talked again. That's why she had stopped.

But what could he do now? Should he talk? Then he would continue to ignore her orders. Should he keep quiet? Then she wouldn't scratch him. He was desperate but decided to keep quiet.

A moment later, he felt her hand on his chest, scratching the pain away.

He sighed with relief.

"You know, we might be starting to get a confession," Regina said casually. "You still owe me a confession!"

"What confession?" Andrew huffed and puffed.

At once, her hand disappeared again.

"Excuse me! I'm sorry. I'm sorry. I'm sorry, I'm sorry. Please don't stop!" Andrew begged for mercy.

"You're talking again! But I don't want to be like that. When you ask for forgiveness so nicely, I just can't resist." Regina chuckled.

She scratched his chest again.

Andrew couldn't take it anymore. He hated Regina. Not really, but he kind of did. He hated her. He hated the way she held him and could do anything she wanted with him. And she did. He'd never been so dependent on anyone else's kindness before. It drove him crazy.

FEMDOM PART 2

He seemed to be nothing in her hands.

Regina laughed, made fun of him, humiliated him, and he thought that was cool, too.

"Let's get to the end. I'm getting bored. I've understood by now how easily you can be influenced and how weak you are!" Regina mocked.

That beast!

Helpless rage rose up inside him, but he said nothing. He didn't want her to stop.

"I have to get something out of my bag. So I'm going to stop scratching for a while. Don't worry. We'll be right back." Regina said jubilantly.

Her hand disappeared, and she was digging in the bag. The itching returned immediately, but her promise helped to take it off.

"I'm afraid we'll have to break another one of your clothes. I hope you don't mind!" Regina teased seductively.

Andrew only had his shorts on.

Actually, he would've been happy to see her get into it. After all, he had already undressed in front of her, but she hadn't seen him naked yet.

But at that moment, he had no good intentions.

FEMDOM PART 2

The cold steel of the scissors startled him, but with practice and with one hand, the other rubbing his chest again, she cut the cloth. He felt the draft expose his flaccid penis.

"It's not really that big, I think. What do you think? I've seen bigger." Regina teased again.

She stopped her scratching for a moment to give her words more impact.

What could Andrew say? He had to endure the shame. He had always been quite content with the size of his little friend. Not that he made any big comparisons, but the inconspicuous size comparisons in the changing room at the swimming pool had always left him feeling good.

"It's not uncommon for your girlfriends to be unhappy with your performance afterward, right?" Regina mocked him again.

Andrew replied nothing.

"Do you ever advise them to bring a dildo if you want to sleep with them? So they can get something out of it?" She laughed. "Well, let's get on with it!"

She tugged at his shredded underpants, and he lifted his hips so she could pull them away rudely from under his butt.

Now he was completely naked and defenseless in front of her.

And he was ashamed.

FEMDOM PART 2

"I'll give you three choices. A, B and C. And you get to choose. I think that's fair. A. I'll warm up the wax and we will do a full-body waxing. Legs, chest, arms, armpits, between your legs. Advantage: I'm sure the itching will disappear from the nettles. Second advantage: It will certainly do the size impression good if your thing doesn't look like a worm in a bird's nest. I'm sure he'll look bigger as a naked mole-rat." Regina breathed out.

She took a little break. "I think I'm fucking hilarious. How are the nettles, by the way? Are they still having an effect? Should I refill it?"

Andrew shook his head violently. "Please don't!"

"Option B, I'd like to add more. Very quickly, a quick wishy-washy all over your body. It won't take ten seconds. I've heard that it's especially effective on mucous membranes. Like on your little dick. What do you mean? Do you want to try this? I'm sure it'll be an exciting experience. And then I'll go to the kitchen and make myself a nice tea. Then you and I will have an experience together. Do you have any tea?" Regina asked seductively.

Andrew shook his head.

"Well, then I'll just go and buy some afterward. You can enjoy the effects on your skin now. It's supposed to perk you up. I read it's good for acne too." Regina commented.

Could she really mean it? He didn't know it, but he didn't rule it out anymore. On the third option, her voice sounded icy.

"Option C: You tell me how many times you played with yourself behind my back. Then you accept your punishment, which will certainly not be pleasant, but far less severe than option A or B. What do you say? I just want to hear one letter from you. No whining, no begging, no whining." Regina spoke sternly.

"C, C, C!" Andrew screamed.

What else could he say? He didn't really have a choice.

"Oh, interesting! I would have thought you'd choose B. Or did I get you wrong?" Regina laughed wickedly.

"No, C. C is right!" Andrew pleaded.

"So, tell me," Regina ordered.

It wasn't that easy. He didn't know. Often, more often than usual, anyway. He guessed.

"A dozen times," Andrew replied.

"Wow really? A dozen times! Twelve times you played with yourself, and not once did you think to ask permission? Even though I asked you?" Regina asked commandingly.

What could he say? It was like this.

"You realize you'll be punished for this. You cheated twelve times. Twelve hits are more than adequate. I would have expected once or twice, but you've obviously had nothing else to do these past few days but hold your dick!" Regina admonished.

"But you promised me it wouldn't be so bad!" Andrew pleaded.

Andrew felt helpless and totally unfairly treated. Regina couldn't do that!

"I didn't know then how big a betrayal you were. I'm so disappointed with you. I'm going to tell you how it's going to go. You'll take your punishment like a man. All twelve. I'll make it nice if you cooperate. Then I'll do something else to make sure this doesn't happen again. After all, I can't trust you. I think we agree on that. And then I'm gonna cut you loose. Spit will help with nettles. But I don't suppose you could put enough spit together to rub your whole body. Besides, vinegar and cold water will help. I have a bottle of vinegar essence here. You can have it. I suggest you cooperate, keep still, then everything will go smoothly and you'll get your salvation!" Regina spoke authoritatively.

Andrew swallowed.

He shuddered at her sadism, which she displayed. 'I'll do anything you want.' This sentence now sounded bitter and fatal. But what could he do? He could of course end it. This was her game and he was her toy. But would he end it forever? Not a chance. He quickly pushed that thought far away from him.

FEMDOM PART 2

His head was heavy, and it took some effort to overcome it when he finally nodded.

Before Andrew knew it, Regina had very quickly stroked his upper arms, forearms, thighs, lower legs, left and right chest, and belly.

"That was eleven. I spared your little friend! So you still owe me one! If it happens again, you'll get the twelfth, and he won't be so kind and brisk! Understand?" Regina asked.

"Understood," Andrew replied.

She was digging in her bag, and at that moment the itching started.

He couldn't say where it started, there was no place worse than another. Again and again, another part of his body would call out to his brain in distress.

And while Andrew felt his body burning, it tampered with his penis. He didn't know what Regina was doing; the itching robbed him of every clear thought.

Once she admonished him, "Quiet! Don't move so much! It'll just take a lot longer."

Then it clicked.

He later remembered the sound that sounded so fateful. But at that moment, there was only the burning on his body.

A moment later, Regina had released his shackles.

FEMDOM PART 2

Andrew tore the mask from his head.

The glistening daylight stabbed him in the eyes. He jumped up from the bed as if stung by a tarantula, grabbed the bottle of vinegar essence she was holding out to him, and rushed into the bathroom. He turned the shower on full blast, and cold water cooled his body. Then he fiddled with the bottle, unscrewed the cap. The stench of vinegar poked into his nose. He didn't care. He poured the stuff over his body and rubbed it in. It burned a little, but it neutralized the much worse burning of the nettles. He kept to himself for quite a while.

****

In the meantime, Regina packed her things together, and then she went into the bathroom and looked at Andrew, who was crouching in the shower and rubbing wildly all over his body. It looked funny.

She hung the chain on which the key to Andrew's chastity belt hung around her neck and then left his apartment. Andrew obviously had enough to do with himself to realize what was dangling between his legs down there.

Chapter 25

MANUVER CRITIC

Regina could not deny it: she had gone damn far. Too far? She hadn't planned the twelve strokes with the nettle that way. But she had been really angry that Andrew had cheated her so brazenly.

It had actually been planned so that she herself wanted to soothe his burning with the vinegar essence. It was supposed to be something like carrot and stick. She wanted to be his nurse and his dominatrix. All at once. But then the fury took hold of her.

She didn't think it was very elegant how he had rushed out of bed stark naked and into the shower like a wild man to relieve his agony. She hadn't really wanted to go that far. Had it all been a bit too much? Had she gone too far?

Regina was a complete amateur, after all. Nobody could really blame her for not getting it all right.

"Was Andrew angry? Would Andrew drop her now, like that dominatrix Angela?" Regina wondered.

She thought with horror about how she would have to find a new flat and drag all her furniture down the stairs again. No one would help her this time. It would suck.

FEMDOM PART 2

Fuck it!

Maybe it didn't come to that.

Maybe Andrew had enjoyed it.

Anyway, it had been a lot of work to research all this.

Regina only came across the nettles by chance, but then she was interested. A forum on the Internet reported about it. So she researched nettles, read Wikipedia articles, and tried to find out how harmful the formic acid that caused the itching was. Finally, she didn't want Andrew to get any allergic shock. She didn't want to have to explain to the emergency doctor why Andrew was chained naked to the bedposts and in stinging nettle shock.

She now knew a lot about nettles.

Well, Regina kept the thought in mind. It didn't seem so attractive to her to mess around with Andrew's little friend, though.

She hadn't gotten that far.

Although, of course, she had gone much further than that.

The chastity belt thing happened to her more by accident.

"What there was everything?" Regina thought back.

At Amazon, she had fought her way through the reviews of various models, had read about advantages and disadvantages. There were huge communities on the internet dealing with chastity belts for men, and when you read like this you could get the impression that every second man was kept in check like this by his wife.

Regina had hesitated whether she should order such a thing. After all, it meant that she would have complete control over Andrew, and she was not really interested in that. But then, after a long struggle and weighing the pros and cons, she had decided to give it a try. She didn't have to keep him in it for months, as some women seemed to do with their husbands. She had thought of it as a game that was finished after a few days.

After all, it also had something to do with hygiene.

Actually, Regina was quite pleased with herself. Everything had gone according to plan, and she had lured Andrew out of his reserve. Maybe she had gone a bit too far in the end. But it was not all that easy!

****

While Regina was at peace with herself, Andrew was shocked.

He sat on the couch in his bathrobe and thought. His body had calmed down again, but he was still exhausted. Actually he had wanted to work, but that was out of the question. Not after this.

"Who had I gotten into trouble with? Was Regina just perfect or completely mad?" He wondered and wasn't so sure what he had just experienced. It had blown him away. Regina had really stretched his limits.

It was already crass.

"But did Regina know what she was doing and was it all still okay? How do you get ideas like nettles? It wasn't normal. How she played with him, lured him out of his reserve, how she manipulated me, was nice and friendly like a little angel one moment and mutated into a cold witch the next." Andrew thought. She definitely scared him. He had the feeling that he was messing with a force of nature that would crush him one day. Like one of those extreme surfers who only picked out the biggest killer waves and played with their lives every time until one day, they were swallowed by them and never spit them out again.

Andrew could have stopped it, but like a surf junkie, he wanted more. He wanted to go on. And if at some point Regina swallowed it and never spit it out again, that was fine too.

But it wasn't just that that bothered him. His dick was stuck in a plastic tube that was really tight and wouldn't let him move. The whole thing was secured by a small padlock. For a bolt cutter that would be no problem. His expert eye saw that immediately. But did he want to use a bolt cutter in this most sensitive of all body regions? Not a chance. He certainly wouldn't do it himself, and he couldn't ask anyone else to cut the thing away from him. So he had no choice but to play the game. He had gotten himself into that kind of trouble, and it wasn't unpleasant either.

Andrew's only problem was that he couldn't get it up anymore, but he had to think about it all the time, because this plastic part could be felt all the time, and so his dick tried to get hard all the time. It was so bad that he couldn't think of anything else.

But no matter what he tried, he couldn't reach it with his fingers to get some relief. It was disgusting. "How long could Regina keep me locked up in there?" Andrew had already realized that it was still possible for him to pee, so that was no reason. But still!

This is not how he had imagined it all. That she took it all so seriously.

Well, he didn't have a choice, for now anyway. He had to play along. He'd see it athletically and show her how long he could hold out without her permission. She would see it! It was important to him, a way to get his self-respect back and to show her that he could take this abstinence like a man.

****

Meanwhile, Regina had another problem. She sat together with Michelle and Laura in the cafeteria of the university and they laughed wildly. Michelle and Laura told her about their night after the disco; Laura about her Latin lover, Luke, and Michelle about her little blonde, Mandrake. They had obviously told the stories more than once because they

FEMDOM PART 2

knew their respective punch lines. Regina was sure that the Latin lover wasn't as pathetic a lover as in Laura's story, and the little blonde was certainly not such a great stallion with such a huge part that one had the feeling of being torn in two, as Michelle explained quite frankly and with quite a lot of details, maybe too many. Of course, it was fun to listen to the anecdotes and it was fun to bitch about the guys.

But then Regina's problem started: She would have loved to tell about Andrew. What she did with him, how she made fun of him to the point that he did everything she wanted. She would have loved to take them home with her. Then they would have rung Andrew's doorbell, stormed into his apartment. Regina would have chewed him out in front of them and then she would have ordered him to undress. She would have loved to see his face, how it alternately turned red and pale, how he swallowed, and begged her with her eyes not to ask him to do that. She would have told him aloud not to make such a fuss, and he would have finally given in. She would have given so much for the look of her friends when they saw the chastity belt for the first time. The two girls would have laughed so hard they couldn't breathe. And as she had met them, they wouldn't torch long. They would throw themselves at Andrew and make fun of him. They would try to make him horny and then make fun of his limp, trapped little worm. They would laugh limply and Andrew would sink into the ground in shame. And at the same time, he would be so horny! She could imagine how hot it would make him.

FEMDOM PART 2

But Regina couldn't do all that. Andrew had made it clear to her that discretion was his biggest priority, which she wasn't allowed to cross under any circumstances. And that's all that was left to her. She was sure that coffee and her pad would give her a bunch of great ideas on how to make Andrew even smaller with the help of her friends. But all this was completely out of the discussion. He wouldn't go along with it, even if she put a Sado-masochistic leather mask on him. It would be too risky for him, and she could understand that. Regina herself didn't want to be seen like that. As a dominatrix. And as talkative as Michelle and Laura were, as much as they loved blasphemy, Regina wasn't sure that she herself could not become a subject of conversation very quickly. And she didn't want to be considered as a crazy bitch for the best of reasons. Then she would rather have the image of the slightly uptight one, which she now had, making excuses to avoid one-night stands.

But despite everything, it was burning on her nails and on her tongue. Regina thought about how she could put her story into the mouth of someone else, "Something really crazy happened to my neighbor's daughter the other day! She met this guy..." But first of all, it was too transparent, and even if she got away with it, it would sound lame to tell about other people to whom something cool had happened. "It just showed how casual and reckless you were," Regina told herself.

In a funny way, she found herself emotionally connected to Andrew, who was certainly full of clients now, to do his part, but couldn't do it anymore. Exactly the same way

FEMDOM PART 2

Regina couldn't talk about her great successes with regard to Andrew.

Regina could still register in her Sado-masochism forum and brag a little bit there, but probably those who had been doing this for years could only smile tiredly about their small successes. The internet was not her solution.

Regina and Andrew, both were prisoners of their history. They did such great things together, but they had to keep them to themselves.

God, why did it have to be so complicated? Secrets! If only they didn't demand so much secrecy!

So Regina had to endure the mockery of her two friends because she had let Terry, the philosopher, down and had given her instructions that she shouldn't be so prudish. Just as she had made fun of the greatness of Andrew's part without really being justified.

Terry, by the way, had met her again the previous day by chance. In the canteen, she was standing in line for vegetarian food and suddenly he was behind her. She didn't recognize him at first but reacted to his greeting. In normal light, he looked actually quite nice. Tall, with a fluffy hairstyle, a little worn out, probably to underline that he was not so materialistic. She liked the three-day beard.

"Do you like veggies?" Terry asked, and without waiting for an answer he said, "I knew that right away!"

FEMDOM PART 2

It didn't surprise Regina that he was vegetarian, probably even vegan. He had nothing on his tray yet, so she couldn't be sure. Such a philosopher was convinced that all animals have a soul, too, and then one could hardly eat it. Regina, on the other hand, was only in the vegetarian queue, because it took too long for her with the goulash and the bratwursts. It had quickly become too complicated for her to be a vegetarian.

Anyway, they got into a conversation and Terry told about the pitfalls of the right nutrition. And because Regina didn't want to poison the conversation by her carnivorous preferences for schnitzel, she nodded here and there as if she knew these problems exactly. When she revealed her little knowledge that there were also vegetarian and vegan ready-made products that were not healthier than the ready-made products for meaties, as she called them, Terry only looked horrified.

Regina couldn't really interpret the look.

She was anxious not to interpret Terry's nutritional fundamentalism negatively.

But during the whole conversation, she had the feeling that the next sentence Terry uttered would expose him as a total asshole.

But this didn't happen. He remained nice and also quite funny. But Regina couldn't get rid of this bad feeling that there was an idiot in him who was just waiting for someone to let him out.

FEMDOM PART 2

Suddenly, Regina had this fantasy in front of her eyes, how she was sitting with Terry at the table of the canteen, in the middle of the vegetarian department. He had the vegan vegetable pesto on his plate, and she had the Wiener schnitzel with fries.

Regina was annoyed by his do-goodness. He babbled and babbled and babbled about the poor animals who suffered when you ate meat or cheese or wore leather. He just couldn't stop.

In the middle, of his lesson about cruelty to animals, while keeping fattening pigs, Regina finally got fed up. She jumped up and wiped his tray off the table. The plate shattered when it landed on the floor and the noodles spilled on the floor. He looked at her stunned and all the other vegetarians as well. Everything fell silent and looked over at them.

But Regina only started now. She was enraged.

"I have had enough of your moralizing, you whistle! You aren't better than me just because you don't want sausage. You are one yourself! Nah, you're even less than that. You're a pathetic little worm!" Regina rebuffed.

Drops of saliva flew out of her mouth, she was so angry!

"You're so pathetic, and your principles are so cheap, you'd eat that schnitzel if you could kiss my feet in return! Do you think I haven't seen you staring at my tits all the time? You're totally hot for me and trying to impress me with your vegetarian radicalism!" Regina admonished Terry.

He looked at her in awe. The whole room was looking at him. Everyone was curious about his reaction.

He swallowed and writhed and then his reaction came so quietly that Regina let him repeat it loudly, "Would you allow me to do that? ... That I may kiss your feet? ... Really?"

Regina grabbed Terry by the collar and pulled him over the table.

"Come on, climb up here! Come on, climb up here. Let everyone see what a poor figure you are." Regina commanded.

Soon, Terry was crouched on the table in front of her tray, huddled like a beaten dog.

"And now eat my delicious schnitzel!" Regina ordered sternly.

Terry looked at her with disgust, but also with an irresistible willingness to do it.

"Do it! Eat! Then I'll let you kiss my shoes! That's all you'll ever get from me!" Regina rebuffed.

Under the tense gaze of the entire refectory, Terry bent his head over their plate, took the schnitzel in his hand with pointed fingers, and bit into it.

FEMDOM PART 2

"That's the way you should do it! Eat my schnitzel! Eat it completely, you worm! This pig is dead to you! Show him the respect he deserves! You don't deserve the airy, golden-brown breading that so delicately bulges from the wafer-thinly beaten flesh!" Regina spoke sternly.

Increasingly turned on, Terry bit off ever-larger pieces of meat, barely chewed, but swallowed greedily.

The crowd around him howled. Regina looked around. It was mostly women, of course, because women were vegetarians most of the time. Moreover, the lesbian student union held its weekly meeting. So there were a lot of purple Wallawalla clothes and more leg hair than in a Neanderthal museum.

"Show him!" they cheered Regina. "Not the pig is the pig! The man is the real pig!"

When Terry, the Philosopher, had the schnitzel open, one of the women rushed to him. She had fished a bitten bratwurst out of the garbage. She put it in Terry's mouth and pushed it in and out as if he was forced to have oral sex.

"Take that, you pig!" She ordered.

Terry let it happen, even swallowed the sausage, and when the women's libber got on the table, he licked her toes in the sweaty Birkenstock sandals.

The other women laughed at him and offered him all kinds of leftover meat.

FEMDOM PART 2

"This is your place, you chauvinist pig! At the feet of the women!" they shouted and laughed. Terry, the Philosopher, just let it happen, and in Regina's eyes, he saw how sharp she was that he was forced to do this.

And then Regina was back in reality. Okay, she had imagined it. She got a bad conscience. She had nothing against women's libbers, vegetarians, lesbians, Birkenstocks, or purples. But everything had fit so well.

Regina had to shake her head to get the image out of her head.

Regina wondered a little about these fantasies.

She blamed it on Terry's terribly boring lecture. But Regina was somehow quite fixated on this Sado-Masochism stuff, she had to admit that herself.

Regina couldn't really imagine that Terry was relaxed and open enough to get involved in any games of this kind.

But apparently they had a common destiny that went beyond queuing at the vegetarian counter. Michelle, Laura, Mandrake (the little blonde), Luke (the Latin lover), Regina and Terry were to go to some music festival together in a few weeks. Terry told it as a matter of course, but Regina hadn't heard about it yet. But obviously she had been planned.

The plans for it were probably already quite advanced. Nobody had told Regina about it yet. Regina didn't know what to think. She felt a bit old at that moment because she suspected that people who were three years younger than her were simply more spontaneous in it and made such plans without informing all involved persons about it. Or maybe Regina was not such a real part of the group that she wasn't included in these plans. She didn't know it.

Perhaps Regina spent too little time with her friends?

She saw Laura and Michelle almost every day at the university. But in the evenings, she did something else. She didn't go to bars. Instead, she studied or played with Andrew. Michelle and Laura were much more relaxed about studying. Maybe they were even better at it because they had just left school, or maybe they were still a bit too clueless. Anyway, Regina wanted to finish university as fast as possible. Her two younger friends were apparently less concerned about that.

Was she too much intimate with Andrew?

The games with Andrew weren't so time-consuming. All her research and planning upfront was more like it. It was a welcome change from their daily routine. She was able to plan things out. Andrew didn't contradict. Being a dominatrix was actually a great activity for people who weren't so spontaneous and could use a little reassurance.

Regina didn't feel much like camping, mud, little sleep, a lot of alcohol, bad food, and so on. She actually couldn't imagine that such a festival had anything positive; except for the fact that she had never been to one before and had gone to university to experience something new. Festivals were something new and maybe even something interesting for her. It was something that she yearned to be a part of. So she decided to go and make the best of it.

But Regina wasn't really satisfied with her decision when she cycled home.

She parked her bike in the corridor behind the stairs and climbed up the steps. Regina was tired, maybe she would take a nap for a while, but then she still had to do something regarding her studies. She didn't feel like it. At least there was nothing to do with Andrew at the moment. She wanted to let him stew for a few days. She hadn't yet made a decision on how to handle his belt and chastity. She would think of something.

As she climbed the stairs and passed Andrew's door, his door opened instantly.

Andrew only pretended not to notice her, "Oh sorry! I didn't see you! I was on my way to my office to get something."

"Alright!" Regina said briefly. On her part, she was a bit nervous but more curious about how Andrew would react, whether he would tell her that she had gone too far, whether he would even throw her out. But she recognized very quickly by his appearance that he wouldn't give her the notice. So she could relax.

Andrew was wearing jeans and a shirt. Regina casually looked at his crotch. It seemed to her that the bump was a little bigger than normal, but otherwise, the chastity belt didn't stand out. It wasn't really a belt, but more like a small plastic part in which the penis was placed in a flaccid state and then closed so that it couldn't expand. Actually a clever idea. Who would like to come up with such an idea? Anyway, she couldn't see it under his clothes.

Regina stood opposite him for a moment, but Andrew said nothing. Then when she took a step to walk past him, he said hastily, "What else?"

"And what else?" Regina inquired back.

"Yes, I mean, did you have a nice day at university?" Andrew asked.

"Did I have a good day? Sure. It was great. Really cozy and nice. They handed out teddy bears in the lecture hall, and then we all got to pet some koala bears and feed them lollipops. At the end, there was a pillow fight. It was very nice today! Could be this good all the time." Regina mocked.

It might have been a bit more biting than she intended. But she felt like a fool running into Andrew here by accident. If he lay in wait for her like that, then he was apparently already hot again.

"Did you have a nice day too?" Regina asked and sat down afterward, not to sound so cold, "Did the shower help? How's the cage?"

"Everything's fine again. I can't complain. That was already..." Andrew faltered.

FEMDOM PART 2

"Nice?" Regina offered.

"I wouldn't call it beautiful. Intense, more like...or something." Andrew was embarrassed.

She had to smile inside at his embarrassment. That thing between his legs seemed to unsettle him to the core. But on the other hand, he seemed too fine to talk to her about it directly.

"When will I see you again?" he asked casually.

"You, I don't know. I don't think in the next few days. I'm really very busy. Maybe this weekend, but I can't promise you that. I'm really busy right now." Regina countered.

"I'm just talking about accounting." Andrew countered back.

"Is there anything new?" Regina inquired.

"No, no. I just want to show you some suggestions I've been working on." Andrew stated.

"Well, they're not going to run out on us, are they? I'll just get back to you. Shall we do it that way? Nice!" Regina replied.

With that, she ditched him and started on the final steps.

After all, it wasn't her problem that he couldn't go on. And anyway, Andrew could just get down on his knees and whimper. Maybe she would listen to him.

FEMDOM PART 2

All right, after a few hours of being locked up, it was a little early. His fault.

But when Regina made her dinner and tea, she felt a little sorry for him. Somehow she had developed a pride she didn't understand. Well, people were complicated, and Andrew was right, of course, that he had his quirks.

When she finally sat over her books, she couldn't help thinking about Andrew, how he was dealing with his imprisonment now, and probably couldn't think clearly.

She thought about going down to him, playing some kind of game with him, maybe giving him a cum and then forgetting the belt. But on the one hand, she should have planned all this; on the other hand, she didn't feel like it. Andrew would survive it, and he wouldn't have to wait until the next week.

It had been an empty threat.

FEMDOM PART 2

CHAPTER 26

BEDDING

While Regina had put her legs up and sat in front of the TV with too much ice cream with caramel and peanut cream, Andrew almost went crazy. He couldn't think of anything anymore. He had tried it. He had tried really hard. He was trying to distract himself. He'd had a cold shower. But now that he was no longer free, now that he was trapped and could no longer control his erection, he could think of nothing else. He hadn't kept a record of the number of his autoerotic gimmicks, but he was sure that it didn't happen as often as he wanted to now. And that was only because he was no longer allowed to. Andrew was only aroused, that was definitely not nice anymore!

Anyway, it didn't go on like that.

Andrew had to work. He had to finish a design for the interior of a restaurant. So his celibacy had a negative effect on his business. He couldn't let that happen. He had to think clearly.

Every second was his thought in his step. Every second he felt the thing pulling at him, it was horrible!

Andrew couldn't work like that.

FEMDOM PART 2

So he did what he didn't want to do, what he wanted to avoid at all costs.

He took all his self-respect, piled it up neatly and neatly, and then he threw it in the bin. It couldn't go on like this!

He started the walk to Regina's apartment and rang the doorbell.

****

She took her time. Who else would be ringing her apartment doorbell at this time of night other than Andrew? And what could he possibly want?

"I think it was pretty obvious." She didn't have to amuse herself regarding that.

"Coming!" Regina shouted in the direction of the front door, but she stayed sitting for another minute, stuffed a spoonful of ice cream in her mouth, before she very slowly stepped to the door and opened it for him, "Oh, this is a surprise! I didn't expect to see you here!"

"May I come in?" Andrew asked irately because Regina had spread herself in the door frame and blocked his way.

"What's up?" Regina asked.

"Not here in the staircase. Come on, let me in!" Andrew pleaded.

FEMDOM PART 2

"Come on? Someone is nasty! If this is your attitude, we'd better wait until you're in a better mood! What do you think?" Regina remarked furiously.

"I beg your pardon! But I really must talk to you!" Andrew pleaded again.

"It's been my experience that you don't really need to do anything this late at night. And I don't need to do anything at all. People are too much trouble. You have to find time to relax." Regina chuckled.

****

Regina's played calmness and her know-it-all attitude made Andrew furious. But he could hardly shout through the staircase that it was about his chastity belt, which he could no longer bear.

But that was what she expected him to do.

"This is about that thing downstairs," Andrew pleaded again.

"That thing"? Do you mean my bike under the stairs? What about it?" Regina teased.

"Your bike? No, damn it!" Andrew was getting impatient.

Regina held her outstretched index finger in front of him, "You're so angry again! I can't take it so well right now! Maybe it'll be better tomorrow?" She looked at him with a crooked head as if it was a serious suggestion.

FEMDOM PART 2

Andrew gnashed his teeth.

"I'm sorry again. I apologize again." Andrew begged.

She looked at him silently.

"It's about the belt, the chastity belt," Andrew whispered.

"Oh, the chastity belt!" Regina said a bit too loud for his taste. "Why didn't you say so? What about it?"

"Let's discuss this inside, please!" Andrew was almost in tears.

"Yes, if it's so important to you, please come inside!" Regina spoke playfully.

She opened the door and Andrew slipped through the door into the small living room.

Regina followed him, dropped herself on the sofa, and looked at the TV.

Meanwhile, Andrew stood in the living room as ordered and not picked up. He didn't want to be impertinent and sit down. Obviously this conversation would not become so easy.

"Do you think you could turn off the TV for a moment?" Andrew asked sheepishly.

Regina didn't answer at first, looked at the screen with fake interest, and finally answered, "What do you think? The television? Oh, sure!"

But she didn't turn it off; she just turned it off to mute. The picture was still flickering in the background, and she kept glancing at it to show him that he couldn't count on her undivided attention.

"Okay, all right. It's about the belt. The chastity belt! It doesn't work like that!" Andrew babbled.

"Can you do me a favor?" she interrupted him. "I hurt my neck a bit today. If you stand there like that, I'll get such a bad tug in my neck. Do you think you could kneel down so I don't have to look up like this!"

Andrew obeyed and she reaped an exaggerated response, "You're a sweetheart!"

Andrew resumed his plea, "It's not working. It's just not working. I can't take this thing anymore. I can't stop thinking about sex all the time. It can't go on like this. I have to work. I have an important meeting tomorrow and I have to prepare for it!"

"If it's so important, you're running late with your preparations. Don't you think so? If you had started a bit earlier, you wouldn't be running out of time now!" Regina rebuffed his pleas.

Andrew could have been furious now because she was the one responsible for his not being able to think clearly! But he kept his mouth shut.

"You must set me free! You... well, you should set me free." Andrew realized he had to watch his choice of words.

FEMDOM PART 2

"Well, it would be super, super nice! Just five minutes. I need to blow off some steam! Just once, it'll be really fucking quick. I can guarantee you that. If you want, you can even watch it."

"Well, that sounds great. Five minutes. Go fast. Watch. That's an offer I can't refuse, huh? It doesn't sound very exciting, to be honest, and I don't have to watch you making out with yourself." Regina spoke wickedly.

Andrew was completely desperate. She just didn't understand how important it was to him, how much pressure it was.

"Please. Please, I'm begging you." Andrew pleaded desperately.

Andrew folded his hands imploringly, and Regina laughed once and then looked back at the TV screen.

"How could he sink so low?" Regina wondered.

He begged.

He had never begged before. He had never begged for anything. It was just to get out of his skin, which he did everything she made him do. It drove him to despair, and it made him so hot. He was so turned on! His throbbing erection was fighting this damn plastic prison, and it only made him hotter! He felt like he was going crazy. That was no exaggeration. He had never felt anything like it, had never wanted to orgasm as much as he did at that moment. And Regina? She sat there on her couch like a little girl, like a student, and she didn't care. She just didn't care. She was watching some shit on TV instead!

He could have strangled her!

"You know, I'd be willing to give you a little pleasure in return." Andrew pleaded.

"You mean... you want to fuck me?" Regina teased.

"If you want... I mean... no. Suit yourself!" Andrew begged.

"You're pretty dashing. Has this method ever worked before?" Regina teased.

"You know what I mean," Andrew spoke imploringly.

"No, I don't, and I don't want to know." Regina rebuffed

She looked at the television again.

Andrew was struggling to come up with a strategy.

Maybe he just wasn't submissive enough. Maybe he just needed to be more forceful.

So he got down on the floor and he crawled up to her.

"What are you doing?" She rolled her eyes. "Okay, okay! Okay, okay, okay. Stop! I can't watch this. You have no self-respect." She shook her head theatrically. "I've never seen anything like it!"

FEMDOM PART 2

She spat the words out in front of him, and Andrew wasn't sure if she was serious about the whole thing. He was never that sure, and he always found himself on the wrong foot.

"All right! You can try and convince me. If you're very good, I might let you talk to me." She raised her index finger. "But just maybe!"

Andrew was relieved.

"Thank you. Thank you. Thank you," he said. "I'll do anything you want.

"You said that before and it didn't come out so well for you! But you must know yourself what you're saying. How about making yourself useful for once? You could clean my bathroom. There are dirty dishes in the kitchen. And a damp cloth to wipe the place down would be a good idea too!" Regina demanded.

Andrew looked at her with a baffled look.

"He should clean?" He thought inwardly. "Was she serious?"

But Regina didn't look like she was joking.

What choice did he have? Andrew nodded and bowed to his fate.

When he stood up with his head bowed, Regina hissed in pain, "Oh, oh, oh! My neck! It's pulling again!"

FEMDOM PART 2

Andrew sighed and sat down on his knees again. Then he crawled into the bathroom.

He found the cleaning utensils, looked at them like artifacts from a strange world, finally filled a bucket with warm water, and poured in a good shot of all the remedies.

"A lot helps a lot," he thought.

And then he scrubbed, wiped, whoosh. His movements were awkward; he hadn't done this often before. In fact, he couldn't remember ever having cleaned properly.

"How far had I come? From being a great, perhaps, somewhat underestimated star of interior architecture to a cleaning man crawling on his knees." Andrew thought cluelessly.

But what was left for him?

He was simply dependent on her.

He had to do it.

He wanted Regina to be happy, because only if she was happy could he be happy. He was dependent on her, and he wanted to be. It was a golden cage he lived in and was in the process of polishing it. And that was all right. He had found his place. If she wanted him to crawl on the bathroom floor in front of the toilet and clean it, then that was the way it was. Then that's what he did. If only he would finish what he started.

FEMDOM PART 2

From the tiny living room, the television resounded again. Some yahoos were screaming at each other. It sounded like RTL2. Regina wasn't watching TV.

Is this what the life of these couples who lived this lifestyle permanently felt like? Andrew was cleaning the toilet; Regina was stuffing ice inside her and watching RTL2? He was happy with it for now.

If only she would keep her promise!

After two hours, Andrew had done his job, as she had ordered. His knees hurt, but the humiliation and the feeling of being inferior to her and dependent on her mercy that was still strong and burned in him.

****

Regina sat only apparently apathetic in front of the TV. But she didn't notice anything of the program. Out of the corner of her eye, she tried to take a look at Andrew, how he was working there. How cool was that then? No more cleaning! She just had to train him to be her cleaning slave.

This whole thing and Andrew had already turned her on. That he threw himself on the floor in front of Regina, that he cleaned her apartment even though she had robbed him of his sexuality! How stupid could he be that he was grateful to her for that as well? It was of course touching how much he cared for her in the vague hope of getting laid after all!

FEMDOM PART 2

When Andrew scrubbed her bathroom floor with a devotion she couldn't show herself, Regina had quickly stolen herself from the couch and taken her pad with all her notes. She had set up a section for ideas that she still wanted to implement. She had even bought a nobler notebook, one by Moleskin, which was quite expensive, at least by her standards. She wanted to give it a bit more style and not sketch her diabolical sexual plans on a cheap block. She had to give the whole thing a little more dignity.

Regina also thought about keeping something like a dominatrix diary in which she recorded everything she did with Andrew. It would have the advantage that she knew what she had already done and how it had reached her and Andrew. She hoped above all that she would learn something about her and Andrew's development. It seemed to her that she had changed quite a bit lately regarding her sexuality and she would have liked to keep track of these changes to find out what that said about her.

Well, that night wasn't about that. She'd figured that at some point Andrew would come crawling back for his belt. In a boring lecture, she had started to write down her ideas. She had a lot of ideas. They were enough for several sessions.

Because Regina didn't want to do anything wrong or improvise amateurishly, she looked at her notes. And she noticed that her fingers kept wandering into her lap while she was thinking about what she would do with Andrew. While she was planning, a new idea came to her. A pretty brave one, actually. And it was a spontaneous idea. She was dealing with a toy she had kept from Andrew until now. Regina had ordered it online with all the other things. It was something like the coronation piece in her collection and she had to admit that she was a bit afraid to use it. It would be pretty extreme. At least within the scope of what she had been so daring and experienced with Andrew. But now she thought about using it differently.

"Should I do that?" Regina thought inwardly.

Her fingers, which kept slipping under the block, advised her to do so. Her mind, however, was in doubt. This was another spontaneous thing that could go wrong. And if it did, it was huge.

She couldn't risk it.

Maybe Plan B, which was much more conventional and less exotic, was better anyway because she had something in mind that would make Andrew take his socks off!

Regina scribbled, stroked out, changed her plan, and was far from finished when Andrew crawled into the living room.

"Finished!" he said proudly.

"You cleaned the bathroom?" Regina asked sternly.

"As you asked," Andrew replied.

"Even the toilet?" Regina peered.

"Of course, and the sink and shower too. And I did the dishes, too, and wiped the kitchen wet. And I wiped the sink with a scouring pad like this. Want to see it?" Andrew babbled.

"Later on. Let's just say I trust you for now." Regina remarked.

"That's very generous!" Andrew replied.

She was silent and Andrew took the initiative.

"I kept my end of the bargain," Andrew spoke.

"I don't remember we had an agreement," Regina said, but quickly added, "But I understand what you mean. We should at least take care of your hygiene, I think. You must stink like an otter down there!"

"I actually took a shower." Andrew was a bit indignant about this suggestion but understood that Regina wanted to take care of his little erection, and of course, that was exactly what he wanted.

"You can't reach down there. I will wash you now. Of course, I have to take a few precautions for my own safety before I release you. Get the chair from the kitchen and put it in the bathroom." Regina commanded.

"As you wish," Andrew replied submissively.

Andrew crawled away and Regina reached behind the sofa where she had hidden her new toy in a box.

FEMDOM PART 2

She picked out the handcuffs and blindfold and her special toy. When she held it in her hands, she wondered if she really wanted to go through with it. She wasn't a hundred percent convinced yet.

Regina stuffed everything into a bag so Andrew wouldn't see it and went into the kitchen. There Andrew came towards her. On all fours, he pushed the kitchen chair in front of him. It was tedious. She thought about whether she should allow him to stand up, but then she found that he could also make a little effort. She closed the door behind her, opened the freezer of the refrigerator, took out the ice cubes, and slammed them into a plastic bowl. She herself had never needed ice cubes before, but when it came to Andrew's chastity belt, she had made some as a precaution. Now her farsightedness paid off.

Under the sink, she found a pair of kitchen gloves, which she also threw in the bag.

Should she really go through with it?

Her heart was beating quite fast and she felt the endorphins and the estrogen tickling in her veins.

Regina breathed in and out one last time and then she opened the kitchen door and went to Andrew with determination.

Andrew had put the chair in the middle of the bathroom. It was tight, but it would work.

FEMDOM PART 2

Regina walked past him, dropped the bag so that Andrew could hear that it was filled with all kinds of things. She leaned against the window and crossed her arms.

"Take off your clothes!" Regina commanded.

Andrew looked at her. His heart started beating faster and the testosterone found its way into his body.

Regina had tried hard to sound cold and she looked at Andrew that her words did not miss their effect.

She liked the way he was embarrassed. It was still an experience. She tilted her head, like a little girl scolding her naughty brother. She didn't want him to forget the age difference between them two.

Andrew looked up at Regina like a doused poodle, but of course, he complied with her request. She thought he was playing a bit too much, a bit too coy, but she liked it, so she let him go. It didn't look very erotic, the way he was kneeling and struggling out of his clothes, but she watched with interest anyway. She was the mistress of the house, after all.

Finally, he was finished, squatting in front of her with the grotesque-looking part between his legs.

She stared at him from a distance.

"You look rather silly with that thing you've got on. I must say that. Well, you can't help it!" Regina mocked.

FEMDOM PART 2

She turned up her nose at him as if he wasn't worth all her attention and then went through the bag.

"I'm gonna take care of you there. I think you realize I have to tie you up so you won't jump me or run away when I let you out." Regina offered.

She held the handcuffs in front of his face, then walked behind him and tied his hands behind his back so that he was tied to the backrest. So Andrew couldn't get up this time.

She wanted to surprise him by putting the blindfold on him from behind, but then she remembered that the order was different.

She stepped in front of him, waved the gloves and said, "I don't want to get anything. Who knows what mushrooms are growing there and what creatures are crawling around down there!"

Regina put on the gloves and stretched them so that the rubber smacked against her wrist, like in the bad movies when the doctor announced an anal examination.

The clapping filled the small room and Andrew swallowed. Then she opened the cosmetics cabinet and took out a small nailbrush which she held in front of his face.

"I think we're gonna get all the dirt scrubbed out of you with that one. What do you think?" Regina teased.

FEMDOM PART 2

Andrew didn't say anything, just stared at the coarse white bristles.

Regina laughed, "You do not look as if you are preparing for a festival of joy. Well, we will see! Let yourself be surprised!"

She looked at him that he didn't really want the surprise. "Okay, here we go!"

Regina leaned over him and slowly pulled the leather necklace from his cleavage where the key to the chastity belt hung.

Had she known that he would come by that evening, she would have worn something more revealing than the washed-out and worn-out T-shirt she had had for so long, which she liked very much, but with which she was no longer seen in public. But Andrew hadn't announced himself, and so she didn't get a provocative look. It was his own fault.

Regina celebrated the pulling out of the key and let it dangle to and fro before his eyes.

"Look at him! All the time he was between my soft breasts! How would you like to kiss them, eh? But not a chance." Regina spoke seductively.

His eyes followed the key as if he were being hypnotized.

"You can't wait, can you?" She laughed loud and hearty like a little girl. "Maybe I'll change my mind again!" She made preparations to put the key back on. "What did you say?

"Please don't," he begged. Andrew couldn't take it anymore.

Regina thought, "He is not playing. He is on the verge of a nervous breakdown."

She laughed, "Then I don't want to be like that. But I don't want you to look at your little wretch." With these words, she put on his eye mask.

Next, she opened the lock on the chastity belt. It was a little tedious with the gloves, but she managed.

At the same moment, when the part opened, Andrew's throbbing erection stood upright.

"Wow, that was fast! Someone's ready for you!" She laughed. "A little horny, don't you think? I mean, a little decency and self-control wouldn't be so bad!"

"I'm sorry!" he whispered.

"Yeah, you should be sorry too!" Regina teased back.

She smeared a little liquid soap on the gloves and massaged his penis. He immediately started moaning and breathing harder.

Regina leaned over to him and whispered softly and sensually into his ear, "Do you like it?"

FEMDOM PART 2

"Yes!" he moaned. "Yes! Yes! Yes!"

"Do you think you have earned this?" Regina teased seductively.

Andrew wasn't thinking. He just nodded.

She massaged him slower and breathed again, "Do you really think you deserve this?"

Andrew nodded.

Andrew was trapped in his own world. Regina knew he was no longer in control of his senses. She could do anything to him; she could ask anything of him. He would do anything if she would just move on.

Regina found it a bit dubious on the one hand but above all, it turned her on incredibly. She had never made someone so crazy. Everything she had done so far, which she thought made a man hot, was nothing compared to this moment. She was sure she was something of a goddess in his eyes.

She paused.

"Please go on, please!" Andrew begged.

"Tell me what I mean to you," she breathed in his ear again.

"Everything, everything you mean to me!" it came out immediately.

FEMDOM PART 2

"I think you should try a little harder. If I mean everything to you, then surely I deserve a little more effort." Regina teased playfully.

Andrew pondered for a moment, and then after a few moments of hesitation, it shot out of him, "You are everything to me! You are... you are... You are the most valuable person in my life. You control me. You decide what I do and don't do."

Regina began to massage him again and to the rhythm of her movements he puffed out the words, "I must always think of you. I cannot help it anymore! You are always there. In the morning, at noon, in the evening!"

Regina was careful. She noticed that he was nearing his climax, so she slowed down again. She didn't want to lose control over him.

"You humiliate me, you force me on my knees, and you command me to serve you. And it's so awesome. So awesome! How you humiliate me, how I lie in the dust before you! It's so embarrassing, but I always want more!" Andrew spoke with all his heart.

His breath was getting faster and faster, his voice was getting heavier and heavier. Regina found it slowly getting too delicate.

"You mean everything to me!" Andrew spoke intently.

And then he said only one word in the rhythm of her movements, "Please! Please! Please!"

FEMDOM PART 2

Andrew was so close to the climax, throwing his whole body into her movements.

Regina watched fascinated. It seemed as if Andrew had completely disappeared in his own world of lust, where everything was heading for its climax.

But she didn't want to clear the way for him. She immediately got a bad conscience when she suddenly stopped and shouted in a completely out of place high voice, "There we go! You've been soaped up before!"

Andrew was dangling in his shackles.

Suddenly, he was hanging in the emptiness. He pumped his hips back and forth to find her hand, but it went into the void and he was called back to the reality where there was nothing left for him.

"No! No! No!" he yelled frustrated into the bathroom, and his voice echoed off the tiles.

"Yes, yes. You are soaped up, believe me!" Regina returned naively as if she didn't understand what his statement referred to.

"Do not stop!" Andrew begged, tugged at the ropes, begged. But she remained ignorant.

Regina just didn't care about his pain.

She just didn't care.

And then frustration broke out inside him.

FEMDOM PART 2

And he screamed, "Oh, God, you fucking bitch!"

And he caught a whistle right away.

"No, buddy. Not like that! You should be grateful I'm keeping that fungus away from you!" Regina rebuffed.

Andrew collapsed in his chair.

He had come so close.

How he hung there, breathing heavily and rebelling against the restraints, Regina was fascinated. She didn't resent the 'bitch' anymore. She probably would have found much stronger words! She was really disgusting. But he wanted it that way. He begged for it. He couldn't complain.

Regina found it fascinating how his muscles tensed up and went limp again when his fight against his shackles was in vain.

He didn't look so bad in handcuffs!

Regina continued.

But now it went on to the second part!

"Let's scrub the dirt away, what do you think?", she whined in a high and completely out of place and casual voice. And then she began to scrub it rudely with a nail brush.

At first, Andrew was still so busy with the relief withheld from him that he didn't notice the torment.

FEMDOM PART 2

But then he felt it. How the hard bristles scrubbed over his sensitive part. Andrew was writhing in his fetters as the disgusting part scraped across his sensitive body.

Regina had to squeeze quite hard but this whole situation made him so horny that she didn't manage to scrub away his erection. He just remained hard and she did not want to hurt him.

His arousal was obviously too strong.

"There, done!" Regina cried. "Now you're nice and clean! Feels good, doesn't it?"

She laughed, and then she slapped a handful of ice cream on his erection.

"Oh God! No!" grunted Andrew in complete frustration.

Regina still had to fight to get him to shrink again.

The whole time Andrew muttered to himself, "No, no, no! What are you doing to me?"

Yes, what was she doing to him? Regina said nothing, but inside she smiled. She was already a fucking bitch. What she was doing to him there!

Regina didn't let herself be put off and finally, Andrew's erection was small again and shriveled up and ready for his prison.

Regina had to fiddle a bit until she had locked him in the chastity belt again.

FEMDOM PART 2

"You can't do that to me!" Andrew pleaded, and his voice swayed as if he was crying.

Regina was not sure. She didn't care. Now she had to decide.

She could just humiliate him now and then let him go, or she could be brave and carry out her plan.

What was there to decide? This whole situation had made her totally hot! Now or never, she thought.

Regina took off the gloves, reached into the bag, and took out the last ominous utensil.

****

Andrew slowly came back from his frustration to reality. He didn't know what was happening to him and what Regina was doing, because she was fiddling with his lap and strapped something on him.

What was that about?

Andrew was confused, but Regina didn't answer his questions.

He heard pieces of clothing. It sounded as if she was taking her clothes off!

Right away, his manhood was fighting against his prison again.

FEMDOM PART 2

My God, if he could only see her! She was so close and yet so far away. A pair of handcuffs and an eye mask took everything away from him. What he would have given if he could have seen her! How much he wanted to see her!

What did she do next?

And then he felt it very close to him and heard it very close to his ear.

She whispered, "So my little stallion! Now I'm gonna have some fun!"

With that, she slowly sat down on his lap.

Andrew felt her naked thighs against his. They felt soft, even though he could feel her muscles.

Her naked arms wrapped around his shoulders and reached into his hair.

Her long hair brushed across his chest, and again electric currents ran through his upper body.

Regina moved slowly up and down in his lap and he felt her breath on his chest and face.

Her muscles tightened and relaxed, she moved, rhythmically on top of him. Slowly at first. Very slowly and consciously.

It was a slow up and down, and Andrew didn't understand what she was doing at first. Except that her breath was getting heavier and she kept grabbing his hair harder and harder and pulling at it.

He imagined what her thighs might look like, always sitting down on his and rising up as if she was riding him.

He himself would have loved to get excited.

Her closeness!

Regina had never been so close to him!

She had never shown so much skin as now, and he couldn't see it because he wore that damn mask!

"How could anyone be so mean!" Andrew wondered breathlessly.

Regina moved up and down and groaned more strongly now, and then she breathed something into his ear, "You're so big and hard!"

It took him a moment to understand. He was neither hard nor tall. His part was limp in a piece of plastic.

"What was she talking about?" Andrew was in a state of frenzy.

And then he understood.

That bitch!

That fucking bitch!

FEMDOM PART 2

She'd tied one of those fake dicks around his waist, and now she was riding him.

While between his legs his own tail, which he wanted so much, which was ready, which could get so hard, was spurned. Instead, she preferred a plastic one!

It was unbearable!

"How could she be like that?" Andrew was baffled.

First Regina wouldn't let him come, and then she sat on him and rode a plastic cock!

It was unbearable!

Had anyone ever punished a person with such contempt?

"Oh, my God!" he stammered. "What are you doing? What are you doing to me?"

"Whine away," she moaned. "This is for me!"

Her breath hot was heavy on his cheek.

Andrew was silent.

He was aware of what was happening. Regina was moving up and down, and he was a passive bystander.

He would have liked to do something to increase her pleasure if he could do nothing himself. But his hands were tied behind his back and his part hung limply between his legs and had no meaning.

FEMDOM PART 2

He was a spectator of her lust.

Uninvolved, unimportant.

He had nothing more to say.

Andrew was reduced to a piece of furniture, completely deregistered.

Regina didn't need him.

He had no meaning for her.

But then she moaned, "Tell me. Tell me again! Tell me what I am to you!"

She was still moving up and down. From the way she shifted her weight, he could tell she was bending her back as if she had found a point of particular stimulation.

Never before had he participated so closely and so uninvolved in sex, never before had he had the opportunity to engage so intensively with a woman's sex. Andrew had nothing to do with himself; he could do nothing but concentrate on her lust. How Regina moved, how she breathed, how she stroked herself.

He had never been so useless.

He whispered, "You are the greatest, you are the horniest woman I have ever met. You are everything, you are my mistress! Nothing like this has ever happened to me before. I am so keen on you. I love you! I desire you! I love you! You're everything to me! You're my mistress!"

FEMDOM PART 2

With his words, Regina came closer to her climax, moaning, groaning, and groaning.

Her movements were even more expressive, heavier, more pregnant with meaning, faster.

Andrew now held his breath.

Her climax was so forceful and then it came over her like a force of nature.

With a sharp scream, then moments of silence and another short scream.

Andrew soaked up everything he could. Her breath, her wheezing, her movements. It was awesome.

He wanted to know so bad, he wanted to experience it for himself!

Instead, he could only guess how it poured over her, how the waves washed over Regina, her body threw itself into it and squeezed everything out of her lust.

In the end, Regina collapsed over him and embraced him. Her naked breasts against his upper body. He couldn't see them, but her hard nipples pressed into his chest.

Her arms around his shoulder, her thighs on his.

He was silent as she breathed heavily and came to rest. He felt her chest rise and fall.

Her sweat rubbed off on his chest.

FEMDOM PART 2

Regina seemed to have passed out, saying nothing, doing nothing, just panting.

When she finally straightened up, her hair brushed against his shoulder.

She felt her breath close to his mouth and whispered, "So how was it for you?"

But before he could say anything, her teeth caught his lower lips and kissed him passionately, and he surrendered to the kiss and gave her everything as if he had a reason to be grateful to her for allowing him to experience her climax. As if he had witnessed something great. Well, he was.

"Thanks for being so cooperative," Regina breathed.

She got off him.

When she took off his blindfold, she had already put her panties back on, but she hadn't covered her breasts yet.

"You're not supposed to live like a dog either," she said smiling and held her breasts in front of his face, and once she pressed them briefly to his mouth so that Andrew could lick over her nipple once.

"Thank you very much," she whispered. "I hope you know that you'll get your turn too. But I want you to be patient. Do you think you can do that?"

Andrew nodded. What else could he do? Somehow this thing had a cleansing effect. He was still under pressure, but things were different now. He could not describe it either, but that had been such an experience she had given him that he tried to bear it. After all, he had no choice.

"Good boy. I am proud of you! Trust me." Regina appreciated.

Andrew nodded again.

And she unlocked his handcuffs.

His muscles ached, he staggered up, got dressed, and left her apartment locked in his cage.

Still, he was proud.

He trusted her.

FEMDOM PART 2

CHAPTER 27

A FESTIVAL OF LOVE

"I'm getting too old for this."

This weekend was Regina's motto.

"I'm getting too old for this."

She was too old for those festivals.

She no longer had to camp in the mud when it was wet. She didn't have to stomp around in the stench of puke and piss to plastic toilets. She didn't have to eat ravioli from a can for three days, which were cold too, because they only brought a small cooker and a small cartridge for six people, which was empty very quickly.

Regina would also have liked to have had a little more non-alcoholic drinks.

But the boys had said that the girls had nothing to worry about. And so there were pallets of beer and only six bottles of water.

Regina put a good face on this game. She tried to joke and to take part in conversations and not to be an arse hole.

But it was not so easy.

FEMDOM PART 2

Regina had the feeling that the three years she had ahead of the others put her into another generation. She found it hard to understand that she could fizz a beer in the morning for breakfast and then at lunchtime you wondered why you felt sick.

Far away, the basses were booming on a distant stage. It didn't seem very desirable to Regina to make her way through the masses of tents, only to fight her way through even more unpleasant masses of people whose hygiene left much to be desired.

Perhaps Regina was too spoiled.

She was definitely too old for that.

For the early morning booze, for camping. All of it.

But that's what Luke (the Latin lover) and Mandrake (the little blonde) were doing. And Laura certainly tried to fit in there and also voted for the beer for breakfast. Michelle looked on it favorably at first, but then changed her mind and took on the role of the bitch who was annoyed about everything. Although Regina had the feeling that of the six she had the biggest aversion to this weekend, she tried to stay constructive and peaceful and soon felt like a mother who mediated between all and tried to find a balance. At times there were arguments over trivialities, then everyone made up, and there was a loud celebration. But it never felt right for Regina's taste. It was always too much: too much whining, too much enthusiasm, too loud, too shrill.

FEMDOM PART 2

In all the bustle Terry had joined Regina's side. He wanted to play the sensible father who called the others to order, the offense was taken by the sausage welded in plastic, but he also always pointed out that there were pig bristles in the Pringles and the bone marrow of pigs in the jelly babies. Regina didn't know whether all this was true, she didn't care much about it. But one day she could no longer hear his grumpy mouth.

But Terry wasn't always like that. He could also be nice, even say interesting things, but he seemed to have the thought that he could succeed with Regina if he pretended to be as bourgeois and fun-hostile as he probably thought she was.

But Regina didn't see herself as bourgeois and anti-funny. On the contrary. She had a guy sitting at home who could tell her how crazy and fun-loving she was. But she wasn't allowed to mention him with the best will in the world.

Regina was just not so childish anymore that she had to get drunk and then ran around bawling. She didn't have to convince herself that she didn't have enough knives and forks, because someone had forgotten to pack them.

Regina hadn't seen herself as a loner so far, but here among all the thousands of celebrating people she soon felt quite alone, like the only adult in a kindergarten of strange children, for whom she wasn't really, but then somehow responsible.

Regina soon longed for her home and wondered what Andrew was doing. His key was still hanging on this leather chain around her neck, and sometimes she would turn it between her fingers and remember that last session in her bathroom.

Regina wondered what Andrew was doing if he was brave and suffered for her, in the hope of one day receiving his reward. Well, there wasn't much else he could do unless he had the idea to pick the lock or go to the locksmith. She could imagine all kinds of things in the relationship, and that's what made it all so exciting.

Regina used the amazingly long period of time when nothing happened to retreat into an uncomfortable camping chair and scribble on her pad.

Laura had already explained to everybody that Regina was a list slut, as she called it, and so nobody was interested in the details.

But the others thought that Regina should plan everything from now on. Regina had politely refused, which surely made her look like a spoilsport. She was quite sure that she could have planned this weekend much better, that they wouldn't have forgotten so much and that they would have had it more comfortable and relaxed if they had thought a little bit more in advance. But one had not.

Dinner didn't become much better by planning either if one had just forgotten the cutlery and had too little of everything but too much beer. Regina didn't feel like leaving the tents of the other festival campers to beg for knife and fork. So she agreed with Mandrake and Luke that they would survive without them.

FEMDOM PART 2

So they got along just fine. It became the motto of the group for this weekend: Improvisation. Regina's motto was still that she was getting too old for such gimmicks.

It was really her!

Instead, Regina developed all the plans in her uncomfortable camping chair on how to torture Andrew further.

There was the idea that she tied him somewhere and left him only one hand free, maybe the left one, and then he had it not so easy. She allowed him to play with himself. If he managed not to cum for an hour, he was allowed to shoot every other day for the next week. But if he did, then chastity was the order of the day for the rest of the week. She was sure that she could make him so horny that he couldn't hold on to himself. These things worked for toddlers, too. One cookie now or three in an hour. The kids always ate the cookie right away. Andrew was no smarter.

Regina imagined her dancing in front of him, teasing and teasing. Maybe she rubbed her body with oil that made it shine invitingly. She would caress him; breathe sweet words into his ear. She would make him decide to have a quick orgasm in an uneconomical way and then suffer from this decision for a week. And when Andrew begged, she would laugh that it was his decision after all.

And on the cue of begging another idea came to her mind. She would lock him up and for every time he begged for redemption; she would impose one more day of abstinence

FEMDOM PART 2

on him. Until Andrew learned that she had him under control and that his pleading only harmed him.

Instead, Andrew was to perform tasks. He should fight for every orgasm. Regina could let him do her chores. She could force him to achieve a certain turnover in his business. She could tell him to lose a certain number of kilos or to do a certain number of push-ups before he was allowed to do it again. She could make him the person she wanted him to be.

But did she want that?

A slave that she could shape according to her ideas? No. It wouldn't make Andrew any stupider. "You didn't have to play this thing all the time." Regina thought.

She needed an intelligent person with whom you could have an intelligent conversation, not about Ray-Ban sunglasses or the right beer. That had been the subject of the last conversation between Michelle, Laura, Luke, and Mandrake. And it had been a big one. Wayfarer or aviator glasses? Regina couldn't tell, but for the four others, it was apparently a question of faith.

Had she been too sadistic?

What she had done to Andrew there was really mean. That she had practically slept with him but he had had no part in it.

FEMDOM PART 2

It made her feel very brave. She'd never done that before. She wasn't really like that. And now she was. Now she was like that, and she liked it.

There was this phrase in the air that he had suddenly thrown at her. He had said that he loved her.

Her intoxication, to be exact, but Regina was pretty sure she heard it right.

"Did he mean it? Did she want him to? To be loved by him? Did she love him?" Regina thought.

Andrew was a funny guy. A little out of touch, a little unworldly, a little spoiled by the wealth of his family. But he had something nice too. He was quick-witted, he was intelligent. She wouldn't have called it love.

If Regina had the choice, she would rather be with Andrew now than with Terry, who was sitting opposite her on a camping chair reading some philosophical yellow Reclam booklet. The others had gone to the stage where some hot band was supposed to play. Regina and Terry had thankfully given up.

Regina looked closer at Terry. He was so not her type. The more she looked at him, the clearer it became. Terry didn't really fit in at a campsite like this. Reclamation books, morals, and vegetarianism had no place here. Neither should she. But that didn't mean that Terry and Regina belonged to the same place.

So between Terry and Andrew, she decided for Andrew.

FEMDOM PART 2

Regina was simply too old for this. And maybe Andrew was too old for her. But it seemed to her that he was closer to her than Terry.

It was complicated, the age thing.

But what did she do with Andrew and his love that came out?

Well, there was always that thing about sobriety and then changing priorities. Regina was hoping that somehow that was true of Andrew as well.

But now she had this key and she could hardly give it back just like that. Not that she wanted to. She was content. For now. But where did it all go?

Regina's thoughts were interrupted. The four came back. They could be heard from far away. Everyone seemed to be drunk.

First, she saw Luke, who staggered up roaring, paused, made a funny face, and then threw up loudly in front of her tent. The three others cheered, Terry shook his head and Regina was so disgusted that she couldn't turn her head away.

She was slowly really ...

FEMDOM PART 2

Chapter 28

ROLLS IN TRANSIT

Andrew had just come home again. He had had his important appointment with a local client. A client wanted to convert an old barn into a restaurant and Andrew was to take over the furnishing.

It was one of the jobs that Andrew had originally put off.

Old barns weren't that kind of thing. He wasn't into retro and didn't expect much excitement. But first of all, it was a lucrative job and secondly, it turned out that this wasn't going to be a bourgeois restaurant for conservative grey pensioners but something hip with traditional German cuisine. And the client had big ideas and an equally big budget.

Andrew had prepared for the appointment for a long time, had ideas about the walls, the floor, the tables and chairs, even the waiters' uniforms, although this was not really his resort.

That was the best part of his job: presenting designs, talking to clients, trying to understand their ideas, putting them into practice, and then presenting them to them.

He could do that, quite well.

FEMDOM PART 2

He could sell and get his ideas across. That was his talent. People could feel that he was serious, that he put his heart and soul into it.

It got annoying when clients asked for changes and they talked to the craftsmen who said that it was not possible. Then everything got complicated and stopped being exciting.

But the presentation of the finished concept, that was what made his job. It was better than seeing the finished product at the end, which was usually a compromise.

Andrew had just presented such a concept.

But with that damn thing between his legs, he hadn't really enjoyed it. His thoughts kept coming back to it. Andrew had difficulty concentrating, and as he walked through the rooms he always felt the look of the owner's wife on him. As if she knew what was under his pants. He just felt that she knew. It was ridiculous and unlikely, but he couldn't shake off the thought that she had seen through him.

The way she smiled at him! That was not the smile that so many women gave him. An appreciative smile. This woman smiled differently.

Well, although he couldn't enjoy it, he had done a good job. The client was satisfied. He obviously had no idea how to appreciate the magnificence of his design. But in return, he had no absurd counterproposals either. The man was completely satisfied, and so was Andrew. The guests would already appreciate his design. The client didn't necessarily have to.

The business part was almost over. For another client, he was still looking for an importer of traditional Japanese wallpaper, but after only a few phone calls he had found a solution for this too.

At the moment the business was going quite well.

He had a little time to take care of the complicated part.

Regina had given him a task before she left for her weekend.

He should think of the next game between them, plan, and prepare it. Planning and organization were his absolute strengths. In all modesty, Andrew was well aware of his outstanding creativity.

Regina had said that she had always thought so much about her games that it was up to Andrew to worry. He could understand that quite well.

Regina probably had the feeling that she got the short end of the stick with the whole arrangement and so she had told him to plan her next session and to take care that especially she didn't miss out and had her fun. This last thing between them had opened new possibilities.

But the task she had given him turned out to be difficult.

How could the slave plan a session that surprised the dominant? He was passive in this matter and she the active.

FEMDOM PART 2

His task was to enjoy, or rather to endure, and hers was to distribute. How could Andrew be the one to act when he should bear it? Such problems were exactly his thing.

Andrew was at first quite at a loss as to how to make it work. He had to admit that he knew very little about her. She was the one who was always one step ahead. She knew everything about him, but him? He could only guess and then he had to realize that Regina was completely different, much more crass and extreme than her blond naivety would have suggested.

Of course, she had given him a list and it limited him quite a bit. "No sex between us!" it said for example.

"I will not walk around naked in front of you!" was another rule. "It's just for my own fun! You have no say in the matter. If I say 'end of the story,' you've gone too far, and the game is over." Regina told.

It went on, the list was long and sometimes a little weird. "No golden shower" was there, for example. Frankly, he couldn't imagine who was going to urinate on whom in this plan. He was irritated that she would even consider such a thing, even if she excluded it from her list. Obviously, she had considered such things. Well, he had it too; he knew what was meant by a golden shower. It was disgusting. So was Regina serious?

Andrew thought it was all very restrictive. He couldn't work like that!

But he had to think of something.

FEMDOM PART 2

Because it was all based on a promise:

"If you're good, I'll let you out of your cage. And if you're very good, maybe I'll let some of your milk of pleasure out too!" Regina teased.

She had smiled mischievously and Andrew had shaken his head over the word 'milk of pleasure.

"I am not a monster. We're supposed to have fun, aren't we?" Regina asserted.

Andrew took it as a sign of conciliation that she wasn't so heartless after all. And he wasn't complaining, either. This was the greatest thing that had happened to him in his life. It was just a little harder than he imagined.

Andrew had spent the day on the phone.

His first thought was that he wanted to give her some kind of wellness day. But he could hardly take her to a spa because her games had to stay among them after all. So he had to do it himself. He had already done the foot massage well.

And he himself had also enjoyed serving her in this way.

With a little more preparation Andrew imagined that he was quite capable of giving her a full body massage. How hard could that be? He watched a few massage porns on the net, but since his personal happy ending didn't come, it was more of a torture to watch and not have any of it.

FEMDOM PART 2

Andrew had managed the last days relatively well. Regina was on her camping trip with some fellow students and so there was no hope that he would be freed. So he had no other choice than to accept his fate and grit his teeth.

After all, she had promised him salvation. He clung to it, even though he was not sure whether he should believe her that all this was also in his interest.

He still drew from their last encounter.

Andrew had never experienced anything like this before. And it was clear to him that he had thought this sentence more often lately. This really was the greatest time in his life. He had never experienced such earth-shattering climaxes.

But back to the planning: In the end, he remembered how he had felt when he came back from his first and only festival. He had been tired, sweaty, dirty, and in a bad mood.

"Why should it be different for her?" He wondered.

Maybe he could start there.

Andrew imagined that he bathed her in donkey's milk while he gently washed her back with a mink sponge if he had to. He wanted Regina to feel like a queen.

And that wasn't just an empty phrase.

FEMDOM PART 2

He meant it. If Regina was satisfied, then he was satisfied too, and his happiness and satisfaction were in her hands. He wasn't quite sure if that was love.

Andrew had said that he loved her, he still remembered that, but he was quite sure that Regina hadn't been receptive at that time and had not registered his words. That was probably a good thing.

For the first time, he now had the vague feeling that the term reached further than between the thighs of a woman.

He had no problem with the general conditions of his planning. He would get something to eat, something light. Sushi from the noble Japanese man on the other side of town.

Andrew researched the price of donkey milk on the Internet, but quickly lost track of it, because cheese made from donkey milk was said to be the most expensive in the world at one thousand Euros a kilo. Maybe it was even a bit disgusting to bathe in real donkey milk. In the Middle Ages, aristocratic women were said to have simultaneously nurtured their skin with honey. That all became too delicate for him. He could not imagine that it was particularly appetizing to pour another glass of honey into the bathtub. He would simply go to perfumery and have the most expensive bath salts they had.

But Andrew couldn't get anywhere like that. He couldn't just dump stuff in the water.

FEMDOM PART 2

He realized that at the latest after googling for the right candles, a kimono for her and traditional Japanese tea ceremonies. Anyway, what did Japanese tea have to do with donkey milk?

It seemed to him that he was on his way to burning down a firework of eclectic knick-knacks that had no style whatsoever.

And Andrew wasn't one step ahead in terms of sexuality.

He needed more than a bath to satisfy her.

He recalled the design philosophies of his interior design idols. How would the Bauhaus school have planned a Sado-masochism session? Or perhaps rather the architect Antonio Gaudi? These were his role models. He would have to follow them.

It was a long night until his plan was finally ready.

FEMDOM PART 2

CHAPTER 29

WELLNESS

"When will you be back?"

The beeping of the Whatsapp-message woke Regina up a bit.

The motorway journey dragged on for a long time. Regina sat in the third row of the family transporter. Next to her, Terry was absorbed in his Reclam booklet. In front of them Michelle and Laura, who had both tried to find a position to sleep. At the front, Mandrake was driving and joking with Luke. It seemed that the two had endless energy or the few Red Bull cans from the petrol station really worked.

Regina passed on Andrew's question to the front. Luke imitated it in the voice of a little child, "When are we finally there?" But Mandrake gave her an answer, "In an hour or so if nothing comes up!"

It was Sunday afternoon, so what could come in between?

The mood was no longer the best. Regina had stayed out of it as far as she could, but especially Laura and Michelle had been upset about all sorts of things. It was all about when they should go back and who cleaned up and how the tents were folded. Regina hadn't said anything but had done what needed to be done. But the two girls were brushed for a riot; they had too little sleep and not enough beauty products to wash properly. Their hair didn't look right and everything was crap.

They all just wanted to go home.

"How did it go?" squeaked another message.

That was a good question. Actually, it was total bullshit. But she had trouble saying it.

"Okay," Regina typed.

"Good bands?" Andrew inquired.

Regina had to think. She had only been on stage once. She was not so keen on music.

"Some", she typed.

"Tired?" Andrew inquired.

"Why?" Regina typed back.

"You can hear," Andrew replied.

"Oh! So you hear." She straightened up.

"How you write!" Andrew pressed.

"Woman lover or what?" Regina admonished.

"Mistress Regina!" Andrew typed back.

FEMDOM PART 2

"Well, well. How's your little boy?" Regina inquired.

"He's relaxed," Andrew replied.

"You too?" Regina teased.

"I am relaxed too." Andrew typed.

"No pressure on the line?" Regina chuckled as she teased.

"Very romantic!" Andrew was somewhat agitated.

"Oh, are you romantic now?" Regina teased again.

"Always. You know me." Andrew wrote proudly.

"I'd guess you just want to stretch your little boy a little." Regina wrote mischievously.

"I'm not that selfish." Andrew countered.

"When was the last time?" Regina asked teasingly.

"I care about you!" Andrew argued.

"Well then. I'm going to take a nap. Long days and short nights. CYA!" Regina signed off.

Regina put the mobile aside but there was one last message.

"I am waiting for you!" Was what Andrew had typed.

She looked at the message until it disappeared from the screen.

FEMDOM PART 2

It was nice!

Nicer at least than the mood in the car.

Although Regina didn't feel like playing games with Andrew; first she needed a shower and then a lot of sleep. And then a proper meal.

Regina clamped her jacket against the window, leaned her head on it, and tried to get some sleep.

When she woke up, the car turned straight into her street.

They were there.

Regina stretched herself. Her body felt stiff and heavy.

She got out, thanked them for driving, and said a not serious, "Thank you. It was beautiful! Must do it again!" took her bag out of the trunk and went into the house.

Regina sighed when she saw the staircase. But she would still manage that. With tired bones, she stomped up the stairs.

When she reached the fourth floor, the door to Andrew's apartment opened.

"There you are at last! I've been waiting for you!" Andrew greeted.

Regina looked at him and then tried to refuse his offer.

FEMDOM PART 2

"You, I don't feel like playing games. Not today. That was really stressful!" Regina rebuffed.

"I understand, but I have prepared a little bit!" Andrew offered.

She sighed, and the next moment Andrew had taken the bag from her hand and pulled it into his apartment.

"All right, all right, all right," she said.

Dozens of candles were burning in the hallway, pointing the way like the lights of an airstrip.

Andrew led her into the living room.

"Wow!" Regina said. "You made an effort there!"

The shutters were lowered and in the living room, there were hundreds of candles that bathed the room in a warm light.

"After all the strobe lights and the light show I thought your eyes liked it rather dimmed at the moment. Unplugged, so to speak. Hence, analog candles." Andrew spoke earnestly.

"Very thoughtful of you!" Regina appreciated.

He led her to the couch and sat her down on it and sighed.

"Just a second," Andrew said and disappeared into the kitchen, only to return a moment later with a tray. Some pieces of sushi were draped on a wooden board, a glass of champagne and one with orange juice was on it, as was another burning candle."

"Another candle!" She smiled. "Let me guess, lest my lighted eyes miss!"

"Exactly!" Andrew smiled back.

"And sushi! Homemade?" Regina inquired.

"Unfortunately not. I guess it's not that easy to get the rice right, and it takes ten years to become a sushi chef. I only had one weekend." Andrew argued.

"And you had to put up all the candles." Regina asserted.

"And squeeze the oranges!" Andrew replied.

He held the tray out to her. "Juice or champagne?"

"I think I'll choose the juice. I could do with some vitamins now." Regina accepted.

"Very well," Andrew replied.

She took the glass and took a deep sip.

"Isn't it too cold?" Andrew sought for an answer.

"It's perfect." Regina appreciated.

"Very nice. How about some sushi? I have the sticks here. They're bamboo, but I didn't carve them myself." Andrew proposed.

FEMDOM PART 2

"Oh, that's too bad! Maybe next time!" Regina stated.

"Would you like to eat it yourself?" Andrew offered.

"My weary fingers would be glad if you'd serve the chopsticks," Regina demanded.

"Very well. The lady would like to be fed!" Andrew teased.

He fed her some pieces, sometimes dipped in soy sauce, sometimes in wasabi.

****

Regina didn't know so much about sushi but it tasted good. She found it amusing how much Andrew courted and courted her. She hadn't prepared anything, was also too tired, felt too sweaty and tired for any kind of game. But it wasn't her job either. She had told him that he should take care of her. Then he should, too. In the background of course there was always his chastity belt and his satisfaction. Now, if Andrew exerted himself a little, she might grant him those. She didn't feel like sex. She just wanted to relax a little. So far, he's allowed her to relax. The sushi satiated her without being heavy in the stomach, and the orange juice was delicious.

"May I suggest we change our whereabouts," said Andrew in his servant manner, which reminded her of a butler.

"Oh? What do you suggest?" Regina was curious.

"The bathroom, if you please." Andrew offered.

"The bath? Isn't this place a bit unconventional?" Regina asked curiously.

"Let me surprise you." Andrew offered.

"Very well!" Regina praised.

He held out his hand to her and she accepted it as help to get up.

"I've done very well on the couch," Andrew spoke submissively.

The path to the bathroom was lined with candles again, and there were at least a hundred in the bathroom too. Andrew had made an effort; she had to give him that. Regina didn't want to know how much work it was to put them away again and scrape the wax off. Well, that was his business.

Andrew had a big bath. Andrew had explained to her that it was modern now. To have a big bath: The bathroom as a spa. Regina had already noticed that he was very proud of it.

It was spacious, had a separate walk-in shower and a huge tub. And this tub was now filled with water, and white foam had formed on the surface. There was a small side table next to it. On it laid a sponge, an eye mask, and a bowl covered with a cloth.

"Bathwater and sponge and eye mask. I suppose it's all for me." Regina asked.

FEMDOM PART 2

"Almost. The eye mask is for me. I thought you could use a bath. A camping trip like this is rarely very relaxing, and you collect a lot of dirt. It might be a good idea to get rid of the dirt. But maybe you wouldn't want me to watch you strip down and splash in the water. You put that on your list. And I respect that. So I'm gonna put on the eye mask." Andrew proposed.

"You might as well just let me bathe alone!" Regina said.

"If you want to, of course, you can. You're totally free to do that. You're missing out. I have spared no expense and effort and have taken a crash course in massaging. Really professional. I now know everything there is to know about massage and what you can learn in ten hours with a trained masseur. My hands are like a black belt in the massage." Andrew offered.

"Oh?" Regina was surprised.

"And just so we're clear, I'm talking about the back and the feet in the first place. Not dirty body parts. So, if you know what I mean." Andrew replied.

"I get it," Regina said.

"The masseur I hired said he didn't do dirty work, and he wouldn't let me practice on him." Andrew expressed.

"But he taught you everything else about massaging?" Regina asked surprised.

FEMDOM PART 2

"Well, at least about the regenerative back massage. If you let me, I'll show you!" Andrew offered.

"It must have cost a lot, a masseur like that," Regina said teasingly.

"The man is a certified massage therapist. I would be doing him an injustice if I didn't tell you. Well, that kind of knowledge can be applied over and over again, I'd say. So it was a good investment. Nothing is too expensive for you." Andrew asserted.

"Did you get a diploma, too?" Regina teased.

"If you want, I'll get it later!" Andrew replied.

"Please do! And what's in the bowl?" Regina remarked.

Andrew took the bowl in his hand, pulled off the cloth, and presented, "Rose petals."

"How noble. Did you pluck them yourself?" Regina inquired.

"I spent last night in the cemetery, picking the petals from the graves. Just kidding!" Andrew joked.

"Now all that's missing is the donkey's milk in the bathwater." Regina asserted.

"I was indeed thinking about donkey milk, but it has slightly stretched my budget." Andrew pleaded.

FEMDOM PART 2

"And you spared no expense or effort!" Regina asked seductively.

"For you, always! Now, how about that bath?" Andrew replied.

"I think I'll take you up on your offer." Regina expressed.

"Very well. Then I'll make myself invisible." Andrew offered.

Andrew put on his eye mask.

"If you want me to help you undress, all you have to do is say so." Andrew offered.

"Thanks, I think I can manage." Regina countered.

It was a little weird the way he stood there. Serving like a butler, but with the blindfold over his face.

Still, Regina he had to get a little carried away to undress in front of him. She still felt dirty from that weekend, sweaty and greasy. Regina pulled the t-shirt over her head and threw it on the floor. She watched Andrew if he could see something, if he could look at her, now that she only wore her bra on her upper body. And of course the leather chain with the key on it.

But Andrew stood still.

And so she decided to go on. She kicked the shoes off her feet, took off her socks, and unbuckled the belt of her trousers.

FEMDOM PART 2

And she was still looking at Andrew carefully. He seemed to react to the metallic rattling of the belt.

She hesitated a moment, then took off her jeans.

It was still funny because Andrew could just take off the eye mask.

On the other hand, he had already seen her breasts, so she could also take off the bra. And he had seen her orgasm. How much more intimate could it get? Under the foam, he couldn't see that she was naked either. So she got out of her panties in one quick movement.

Regina carefully climbed into the warm bath. It was a huge tub. She'd never been in a bathtub that big before. In addition, air bubbles were bubbling out of some jets, which tickled her a bit, but felt good. She only knew something like that from the swimming pool. Andrew had a taste, she had to give him that. And of course, the necessary money to be able to afford it.

The water relaxed her immediately, and Regina sighed a long, long sigh, "Fine!"

Andrew, who had followed her actions with his ears, slowly groped his way to the edge of the tub and then to the bowl with the rose petals, which he spilled over her and which slowly fell into the water. Most of them, at least. Since he couldn't see, some went next to it and landed on the floor.

Regina laughed: "Very noble! I must say that!"

FEMDOM PART 2

She dipped her head under and enjoyed the warmth of the water that surrounded her body and relaxed her muscles. She looked at the candles that stood on the edge of the bathtub, on the windowsill, on the bathroom cabinet, and gave off their light. She was impressed. Andrew had really tried hard. No one had ever done anything like that for her before, and she had no problem with it all looking a little kitschy. Like something out of an '80s video.

Andrew let her go for a while and stood motionless in front of her.

Regina finally ordered a glass of champagne and Andrew groped his way out of the bathroom. She wondered if he would step into the candles but that was not her problem. He came back unharmed with the tray.

The alcohol was quite pleasant after all. Andrew packed them together with the warmth of the bath into a cozy cocoon.

Regina enjoyed it for a while and looked at Andrew who stood there patiently waiting while she enjoyed his blind attention.

He was now really obedient, well-behaved and submissive, didn't moan, didn't want anything from her, at least he didn't show it. What more could she wish for? She could always have a man like that around her!

"I would then be ready. Let your hands do their magic!" Regina proposed.

FEMDOM PART 2

Andrew smiled under his mask. "I'd love to."

He felt his way slowly towards the tub and found her shoulder. He put me on the edge and started massaging her.

His hands slid down her neck and they felt good on her soft skin. Strong, safe, like they knew what they were doing. There was nothing wrong with their eyes. Regina didn't need any hesitation or insecurity now, she needed someone who knew what to do.

Sometimes the hands would caress her body, and then they'd reach out and grab her hard. Sometimes the touches were fleeting, hardly noticeable, so that she got goosebumps, then again almost painfully firm and gripping. "Was this all professionally done by a massage therapist or had Andrew copied this from an Asian masseuse in a backyard?" Regina wondered.

She didn't really care. It felt at least somewhat professional. His fingers on her wet, soft skin felt right. They showed dedication.

On her trip to the festival, she had missed that.

That, someone, was just there for her.

His fingers slipped along her ribs and stopped at the base of her breasts.

Regina knew what Andrew was doing, and she was okay with it.

FEMDOM PART 2

When they were very close to her breasts, Regina leaned back and his fingers slipped a little further than he had intended and touched this gentle curve.

Regina did that a few times, and at some point, his fingers even touched her hard nipples.

Andrew should calmly know that she liked his massage and he should be rewarded a little.

His hands followed the lines of her body, reaching around her body, stroking her belly, and meeting at her navel.

Regina breathed deeply in and out.

No masseur did such a thing, she was now quite sure. But she let it happen. She had missed the caresses.

Regina enjoyed his hands on her body.

She let it happen and enjoyed the attention Andrew gave her. And she thought of the cage between his legs. What he was doing had no visible effect on Andrew. He was locked up in his prison. He was almost like a eunuch in a harem. Only that the eunuch didn't feel anything while Andrew must be full of frustration. At least the eunuch couldn't feel any joy. The eunuch didn't even know what he was missing. Andrew on the other hand knew too well.

And yet, he didn't let on. He stroked it as if it was the most natural thing in the world and it was perfectly alright that he didn't get any of it.

FEMDOM PART 2

Slowly the hormones in her got better and she got in the mood again despite her tiredness and expectation.

This thought somehow made her even hornier. Regina could enjoy, and he didn't benefit, at least not his little erection. "Did he enjoy it too, was he frustrated?' She didn't know it. But whatever it was, she wanted him to feel it even more.

Regina reached back, and at some point, her hands got to grab his hair.

She grabbed hard and pulled his head towards her and then she kissed him. She pressed her lips on his mouth, forced her tongue demandingly against his.

It wasn't really tender or gentle. Regina was just hot and lust-filled for him and wanted him now and she felt superior to him. Her nipples were harder than his part in his cage. She was the mistress of the house, the lady of the house, the dominatrix. All this came suddenly and quite naturally.

Regina wanted to keep control like a servant.

Because somehow he was.

Her neck was stretched back painfully but she still held his head. Like a constrictor, she turned in the tub and pulled him into the tub.

The water spilled over the edge of the tub, and a little later the smoke rose from a dozen extinguished candles.

FEMDOM PART 2

Andrew hadn't expected it, but now their two bodies lay on top of each other and kissed wildly. Regina nestled her naked body against his wet clothes. She tugged at his clothes. Andrew let it happen. He reacted, kissed her, embraced her, pressed her to himself, but for the time being cautiously and restrained as if he must not go too far. He was submissive.

Regina pressed her thighs between his legs and felt the plastic part under his pants.

Her interest was aroused. Regina reached between his legs and fiddled around with the piece. She had never really understood how it worked, didn't pay attention to the details. It was really a devilish part because she felt his flabby penis, which just couldn't get stiff in the curved tube.

Andrew's growing passion, however, didn't stop there. He kissed her breasts, sucked her nipples. He gave her all the attention in the world. She couldn't remember when anyone had ever fondled the small hollow in her throat, but now his fingers caressed her as if it were a wonder of the world.

Andrew found the key around her neck, took it in his mouth, and smiled.

His eye mask had slipped by now, only one eye still covered her. But he kept the other eye closed. Maybe because he didn't dare to look without her permission, maybe because he concentrated on other senses and stayed in his imagination.

FEMDOM PART 2

Regina didn't know it but watched him for a while as he caressed her body with his hands, his lips and his tongue.

Then she grabbed him by the hair, tore the eye mask off his head and said, "Look at me!"

He opened his eyes, and maybe it was the candlelight, but they seemed more beautiful, more luminous.

"Who am I?" she asked him sternly and pulled his hair.

"You are my lady," he moaned.

"That's goddamn right!" Regina asserted.

She pulled him towards her almost violently and kissed him passionately, and her tongue showed him who was in charge and who was in charge.

Andrew let it happen, showed no resistance. Regina felt like a black widow that devoured the male during mating.

Andrew let it happen and gave in.

When Regina had enough, she pulled his head away from her, looked deep into his eyes and pushed him down into her lap. His arms grabbed her bottom and lifted her out of the water until he could kiss her between her thighs.

Immediately he started kissing her down her rosebuds and his tongue penetrated her. The tide had turned and his tongue demanded while Regina let it happen.

FEMDOM PART 2

Regina leaned back, went through his hair, stroked it, and directed him. When she came closer to her climax, she reared up and let her pelvis sink to the bottom of the tub, and Andrew was forced to go under water to continue his love service.

Regina was only vaguely aware that he could not breathe. But she lifted her basin out of the water, and struggling for air his efforts only became more intense, and so Andrew drove her to an explosive climax.

When it broke over her, she pressed her thighs together and pushed him under water again. Her orgasm was so earth-shattering that she got it with the fear.

Her body twitched with excitement, and Regina felt that time around her disappeared like in a fog and she stepped away from the world for a moment; into this sphere of pure beauty, from which one never wanted to return.

When Regina regained consciousness they only slowly reached the things of this world again. The candlelight, the warm water, Andrew between her legs. She was startled for a moment when she wondered if she had harmed him by pushing him under water, but Andrew lay still between her thighs and looked at her. Over her mound of Venus, between her breasts, which were resting flat and exhausted and only moved gently back and forth as her chest rose and fell as she breathed.

His arms were still wrapped around her buttocks from below and resting on her belly. Regina sighed, lay still in the tub for a while and enjoyed his breath on her clitoris.

FEMDOM PART 2

Finally, she was back to reality again, so far that she was aware of the situation. She pulled Andrew up to her, finally opened his pants and tried to pull them off. Wet as she was, she stuck to his hips and so he had to use a lot of force and kick into the water a few times, which caused new waves that put out even more candles. But finally he had at least one leg free.

It would be enough.

Regina pulled the leather strap with the key over his wet hair and opened his lock with still shaking fingers, which was not so easy under water.

When she pulled the tube from his penis and before he could get stiff, she put her fist around him and kept him so limp.

"Look at me," Regina said again and squeezed a little so that his testicles were slightly compressed. "I don't want this to be over in three seconds, is that clear?"

Regina nodded, and she slowly released his penis from the clasp and felt it instantly grow to full size.

Andrew fished in his pants, some of which were still sticking to his leg and swimming in the water, and finally pulled out a condom.

"But you were optimistic!", Regina said smugly.

"I am prepared for everything! One may hope!" Andrew replied.

FEMDOM PART 2

"I want to be really pushed! But I think you won't last long with your backlog of urges!" Regina asserted.

"We'll see." Andrew offered.

"No, we won't see! I don't want to get out of the tub frustrated because you're taking off early." Regina rebuffed.

"Frustrated? I got the impression that you were anything but frustrated!" Andrew teased.

"Still... I have a better idea!" Regina asserted.

She pulled Andrew to her, took the condom out of her hand and put it on the edge of the bathtub. Then she turned him over so that his back was on her chest. She wrapped her legs around his thighs. With her right hand she grabbed his cock and with her left hand she stroked his left nipple.

Their heads were close together and Regina whispered into his ear in a cool voice, "I will milk you now. Nice and slowly. If you manage to resist me for a minute, then you may put the condom on again afterwards and I will get my second time. But if you don't manage it, you'll be put back in the cage, and then I'll be really angry that I only came once today for my pleasure. And I'm sure I'll be pissed for at least two weeks. Do you understand that?" Regina demanded.

Andrew nodded.

FEMDOM PART 2

"Good! Hold your watch so we can both see the second hand!" Regina proposed.

Andrew obeyed, and when the second hand jumped to zero, Regina started very slowly. She grabbed firmly and moved her hand slowly back and forth.

"You think you will make one minute, don't you? It will be a piece of cake, you think. Look, five seconds have already passed!" Regina teased.

Now she twirled her left hand around his nipple, and Andrew moaned.

"But a minute can be long when you can't control yourself." Regina spoke teasingly.

She moved her hand back and forth faster, and immediately noticed him jumping at her movements.

"After all, it's been such a long time since you've done this! So damn long!" Regina breathed into his ear. "So damn long!"

He got goosebumps.

"Fifteen seconds you've got. But I can tell that you get turned on when I blow in your ear." Regina asserted seductively.

She laughed.

Her hand had slowed down a bit, but picked up speed again quickly in the next set. She thought she had found his rhythm and was now forcing it, "You are so completely out of my league. I have you in my hand!"

Andrew moaned.

His chest rose and fell heavily. Her hand went over his chest.

"Please, no!" Andrew moaned.

She laughed, but at first she did not let up, and his moans grew louder. He begged, "Please, no. Please."

"Thirty seconds and you're about to be shot!" Regina teased playfully.

She stopped and he breathed heavily.

"Let's face it, if I want to, I can push myself over the cliff with a snap of my fingers. Just with my words alone, I can push you to the climax!" Regina demanded.

It started again and immediately at a pace as if there was no turning back.

"Twenty seconds left. You can do it! For me! For your mistress." Regina spoke sternly.

She laughed, her left hand stroking his nipples again.

"I like torturing you!" Regina asserted.

She bit his earlobe and squeezed.

Andrew hissed.

"I wouldn't have thought so, but there's something about seeing a man crawl like that and not being able to resist you. Women want to be courted, after all. They want a man to take care of them. And you want to lie at my feet. Ten seconds!" Regina was toying with Andrew's mind and body.

Andrew moaned again, his breath was heavy, he was back to his "please", but his mouth was only left with a mumble.

He struggled.

"They say that men think about something else to last longer. But I bet you can't think of anything but me, my power, and my body, what you just licked!" Regina teased seductively.

Andrew was now very close and she didn't stop, but whispered more forcefully. Andrew just whimpered. She felt his tensed muscles, his legs fighting against the clasp of her thighs.

"Five seconds left." Regina time lined.

Andrew held his breath.

"You can do it. Four." Regina loved to play the rat and cat game.

His whole body seemed cramped.

"For me. Three. For your mistress. Two." Regina was driving her slave crazy.

FEMDOM PART 2

Andrew reared up, bit his teeth. Regina squeezed his nipple as hard as she could.

"And now come for me. Come!" Regina asserted.

A grunt burst out of him as Andrew reached his climax.

His body was filled with a twitch and he pumped out his seed and he flew in a high arc.

Regina stroked his hair with her left hand like an understanding friend. But with her right hand she caught a part of his seed in her palm.

When Andrew sank exhausted on her chest, she breathed, "Good girl. That was very obedient of you. As a sign of my dominion over you, there's only one thing left to do."

She put her hand over his mouth.

He hesitated.

****

Regina saw how much Andrew resisted what she expected of him. But what was left for him? She was his mistress, she could decide that!

Andrew opened his mouth and licked her hand clean.

"Good!" Regina praised, turned his head to himself and kissed him extensively. At the same time she still tasted a little of the salty taste of his seed in his mouth.

He smiled blissfully at her and then sank his head on her breast.

So they lay in the tub for a while.

When Regina felt that the water became cold, she let warm water run after them. When she noticed that Andrew was ready again, she took the condom, put it on him and the two loved each other slowly and this time almost as equal.

When they got cold again in the tub, their fingers were already shriveled, Andrew said, "I have something else for you."

He fished in a pocket of his jeans and pulled out a small jewelry box, opened it and pulled out a gold chain. Then he took the key out of her hand, threaded it in the chain and put it around her neck.

Regina was visibly touched.

Andrew got up, got out of the tub and helped Regina out.

Then he dried her carefully and wrapped her in a thick terry cloth bathrobe.

Finally he fished the belt out of the tub, put it in her hand and said, "I will get the ice cubes."

****

THE END

Made in the USA
Columbia, SC
17 July 2023